TONY EPRILE

A FIRESIDE BOOK PUBLISHED BY SIMON & SCHUSTER INC.

NEW YORK   LONDON   TORONTO   SYDNEY   TOKYO

TEMPORARY

SOJOURNER

and other

SOUTH AFRICAN STORIES

SIMON AND SCHUSTER/FIRESIDE
Simon & Schuster Building
Rockefeller Center
1230 Avenue of the Americas
New York, New York 10020

SIMON AND SCHUSTER, FIRESIDE, and colophons are registered trademarks of
Simon & Schuster Inc.

Designed by Bonni Leon
Manufactured in the United States of America

10   9   8   7   6   5   4   3   2   1
10   9   8   7   6   5   4   3   2   1   Pbk.

Library of Congress Cataloging in Publication Data
Eprile, Tony.
    Temporary sojourner, and other South African stories.
    "A Fireside book."
    1. South Africa—Fiction.   2. South Africans—Fiction.
I. Title.
PR9369.3.E67T46   1989   823   88-33574
ISBN 0-671-68205-9
ISBN 0-671-64596-X (pbk.)

The author is grateful for the generous assistance of the National Endowment for the Arts
and of the Dorland Mountain Colony.

Portions of this work have appeared in slightly different form in *Story Quarterly 13, Issues,
Hellcoal Annual, Welter,* and *Crawl Out Your Window 9 & 10.*

TO THE
EPRILES
AND THE
GREENS

ACKNOWLEDGMENTS

I wish to thank the many good friends whose support has helped make this book possible. In particular, thanks are due to Alice Lichtenstein, my brother Bob, and Bruce Hoffman; to my editors Deborah Bergman, who got the book started, and Laura Yorke, who has seen it through with unfailing enthusiasm and patience. Finally (and most of all), my love and gratitude to Judy Schwartz, who reads and remembers.

C O N T E N T S

* The Spiegelman Family stories

LETTERS FROM DOREEN

Let us begin this story where it ends. Mark Spiegelman is visiting his parents in San Diego one summer—he is out on the West Coast for a friend's wedding—and, as always, he asks about the news from South Africa.

At the time, he and his mother are in the kitchen putting away the dishes. She does not answer him immediately, but instead hands him the gravy boat and says, "Here, you're tall. You put it away." Mark stretches to slide the gravy boat, still hot from the dishwashing machine, onto the topmost shelf. Its warmth —as if the dish is some living thing—is transferred to his hand.

"We think Doreen passed away," his mother says. Mark knew his parents had been worried about Doreen because this past year there had been no Christmas card from her and no response to the eighty rand they'd sent as a Christmas present.

"We got a letter from Irmgard," his mother continues. "She called the Gillins, who said that they hadn't heard from Doreen and that she must have died."

The Gillins were the people who moved into the Spiegelmans' flat when they left the country. "We could use a decent girl," Mrs. Gillin had said. "Can you recommend Doreen?" So Doreen went to work for them and stayed with them until about a year ago. Since she worked for his family for nine years and Mark had been eleven when they left the country, he calculated that Doreen must have worked almost twice as long for the Gillins. Still, in a recent letter to his mother she had voiced her old complaint about Mrs. Gillin: "She never talks to me like you used to. . . ."

"Did Irmgard say anything else?" Mark asks.

"Just the usual—prices are going up because of all the boycotts—especially food. It's not so easy for someone living on a pension anymore. Now that Max is dead, Irmgard really doesn't have much reason to stay in South Africa. She thinks she'll probably move back to Baden-Baden."

A number of his mother's contemporaries, German Jews who fled to South Africa at more or less the same time she did, have been going back to the fatherland to live. Many of them get a generous pension from the German government, as well as money to simply come and visit. The German word for reparation is *Wiedergutmachung*, which translated literally means "making good again." Mark finds this term absurd, a bit of linguistic black humor. There are some things that can not be made good again. They become part of the past, and the world is forever changed by them.

Dearest Mam and Master:

I am keeping fine and family. I got the money at last now they tell me the money is dollars so this end is less

in S.A. they gave me R.36.59 that's what they gave me.
So I say thanks again Sorry I could not send you a
card for Pasach I could not even go to town to get one.
... I don't know how long I will still be with the Gillin's
as the work is too much for me now as they are trying
to decrease the staff the days they don't come in the
servants must do the flat they just to sweep do the bath-
room windows. You must do the stove wash doors walls,
This is what I am doing washing daily ironing, baking
biscuits once a week silver (you didn't have a lot of
silver) there's no lunch hour you must be ready when
they get home with supper, cook for the daughter she
eats here whenever they want to come. My thumb does
not come right from the soap pad all the other fingers
are alright. I hope you are well and family.

Love Dor.

Lately Mark has found himself asking the young
white South Africans whom he meets everywhere these
days, in New York, the Midwest, Washington, D.C.:
"What happened to your nanny?" It is safe to assume
that they all had one.

The usual response is to dismiss the question. It is
one of those things of childhood that have been set
aside.

Some of his South African peers classify themselves
as Marxists and try earnestly to convince him that the
real issue in South Africa is not race but capitalism,
rule by elites. Late one night, Mark is standing on a
street corner in Manhattan's Upper West Side talking
to one of them, Peter—whom Mark likes mainly because he has the same squarish head and mole on the
left cheek as Nigel Asheroff, a childhood friend.

"Of course there were some excesses in the Cultural
Revolution, but that's not the point," Peter expostu-
lates. "The revolution had been subverted by the intel-

lectuals, and they had to be dealt with somehow. You shouldn't swallow everything in the capitalist press ... all those crocodile tears about violinists planting rice.''

While they are talking, they are constantly approached by beggars. ''D'you want me to starve, is that it? You want me to starve!'' says one lurching drunk who has just been dismissed by Peter with a wave of the hand. The drunk is beginning to get belligerent, but he sees other prospects and staggers off in their direction. Mark asks Peter about the black woman who brought him up: Where is she now? How long was she with them? The question annoys Peter. ''I don't know,'' he responds. ''We had one woman, Bertha, who took care of us as kids, but she's gone back to the homelands now. Everyone had servants growing up; that's not the problem.''

A ragged-looking man approaches them. He fits the category of beggars to whom Mark usually tries to give money: his shoes are much worse than Mark's trodden-down sneakers. They are a size too small and he has worn down the backs with the heel of his foot. ''Go away,'' Peter says. ''We're not giving you money.'' But the beggar had noticed the barely perceptible motion of Mark's hand toward his pocket and says to him. ''You would have given me money, man. Come on.''

''No,'' Mark responds.

''You're letting him control you,'' the beggar cries, pointing toward Peter. ''He's stronger than you.''

Dearest Madam,

My self & family are keeping well. How are you & the family hope you are all fine. Wishing you all a Happy New Year & well over the fast. I last time wrote to you that I dont know how long will I still be here at Gardens I am still hanging on as times are so bad. Food, clothing are so expensive that you hardly have

enough for a second helping for the kids I mean Len-
ora's kids they only have one meal a day, and thats in
the evening when she comes home from work. She's
divorced last year, her husband left his job 2 years
back, does not even support the kids the law does not
do anything they keep telling her to hang on. The
Mainzers are on holiday oversea but I dont know
where, they left the end of August I think they went
for 3 or 2 months. Shes stooping since she had the
operation...

When, at the age of sixteen, Mark returned to South
Africa after four years' absence, he immediately got in
touch with Doreen. "Hullo, Mutt," he says in their
first phone conversation. "When am I going to see
you?"

As a child, Mark was always a slow eater, often forgetting the food on his plate while he immersed himself
in reverie. Doreen would sit with him, as his mother
did not have the patience to watch him toy with his
food. As if to make up for his lack of progress in nour-
ishing himself, Mark had learned to read very early on,
and he would read aloud to Doreen from some comic
book while she periodically interjected: "Ag, man,
just eat a little of that pineapple." Doreen's favorite
was *Mutt and Jeff,* and she never got tired of the way
little aggressive Jeff would lure his tall friend into
some new misadventure. They came to call each other
Mutt or Jeff interchangeably; sometimes Doreen was
Mutt, sometimes Mark.

... I have been home for the holiday Johburg is hot
but out there is boiling you open the windows at 4 AM
but still its the same by 6. you open the doors you are
perspiring you are wet.

I am glad you found a nice apartment, I didn't know

how to write to you as I thought you moved knowing
you were looking for a place Mrs. Mainzer had an op.
she's much better now She's swimming daily only she
stoops a little. there's nothing happening at Eden Gar-
dens it's all quiet My family is keeping very well the 2
kids are at school, only the little at home because he's
only 4. Mutt must be a good cook you know he used to
ask whats that you are adding now only he must not
add too much salt & swear....

What amazed him in retrospect was the warmth with
which African adults, almost any African adult, would
respond to him as a child. Walking past throngs of
black men and women in the late afternoon, his over-
stuffed schoolbag banging against his bare calves,
Mark never felt any trace of fear ... even when these
same adults were waiting patiently, handcuffed, in line
to be pushed into the next available *kwela-kwela* wagon
for some pass infraction. There would invariably be
friendly comments about any new possessions or items
of clothing. "Very nice, little master." "*Siyakubona,*
mFaan." "You give me that bag, yesss?" Doreen, on
the other hand, would mock all new acquisitions with
the Afrikaans phrase, *Skilpad het a nuwe doek.* Tor-
toise has a new hat.

Although Doreen was officially classified as a Coloured and so was exempt from carrying a pass, it was
not safe for her to leave the apartment building without some form of identification. When Mark was five
she disappeared without warning for an entire weekend, returning on Monday morning sour and subdued.
She had gone across the road to talk to a friend and
had been picked up by policemen who did not believe
she was Coloured; they thoughtfully kept her from
disturbing her employers with a phone call on the
weekend.

Even the African gangsters were friendly. A group
of them used to regularly play dice in the backseat of
an old and commodious car parked in the quiet cul-de-
sac below Eden Gardens. The gamblers would give
Mark and his friend from the apartment building,
Lenny Mainzer, each a tickey—the thin, sensual 2½-
penny coins of that era—to go play elsewhere and not
draw attention by staring at them. Bribery had its
drawbacks, however, for whenever the sharp-eyed
Lenny spotted the car in the distance he wanted to go
by and claim his tickey, and it was only with difficulty
that Mark could draw him away.

One day they saw the police break up a similar group
of gamblers who were playing excitedly beneath an oak
tree beside an empty lot. A car slowed down and suddenly all four doors were flung open and athletic young
policemen were upon the gamblers, who scattered in all
directions. They watched as one policeman chased after
a wiry African who was running ''hell for leather''
still clutching several pound notes. The policeman
caught up with him near where the boys were standing,
grabbed him by the scruff of the neck, and doubled
him up with a quick blow to the solar plexus. ''Hell,''
Lenny had said, ''I want to join the police when I'm
grown up.'' Mark had seen the smiling policeman give
the handcuffed gambler an additional sharp punch to
the neck.

In the brown cardboard accordion file where Mrs.
Spiegelman keeps her correspondence, Doreen's letters
are easily recognizable. She always wrote on official
blue aerograms, with their prominent injunctions
against *insluitings* and the customary reproduction of
the Provincial Buildings in Pretoria. On his last visit
to his homeland, Mark had visited these buildings,
where enormous tapestries depict the conquering of

Southern Africa by the white man, and where a sculpture of a man wrestling a bull gives rise in the accompanying free catalogue to eloquent musings on "Liberty Curbed." It was odd to think of an elderly coloured woman spending one percent of a week's income on such stationery.

...we don't have a caretaker any more that old Missus Vogel she got killed a boy hit her on the head with an axe she was taking money from all the boy's paypacket, and Efroom too was doing it. The police caught the boy who killed her it was 6:30 in the morning. You remember how Voggie used to shout at the children when they played near the flowerbeds she was always cross but it was not nice to die like that. Shame ...

Mark remembers telling his mother one day how he hated Mrs. Vogel. "She's a lonely old woman," his mother had said. "She doesn't have a husband or any children." What about Efroom, he had asked, isn't he her husband? Efroom was the black bossboy, a ramrod-straight older man with a gray mustache and steel-wool hair. He had the military bearing of a pukka Englishman and had been "up North" during the Second World War. He issued harsh, peremptory orders to the servants employed by the apartment building, punctuating his commands with a flourish of the stout wooden cane that he always carried. One day when the family was chatting in the kitchen, the evening paper was thrust through the partially open door, leaving a bloody smear on the stove and landing on the floor with a thud. Mrs. Spiegelman pulled open the door and the newsboy half tumbled in, apologizing profusely. He had ridden upstairs in the elevator instead of taking the back stairs and Efroom had hit him on the head to teach him a lesson. Mark's mother washed his head with a cloth that she dipped in an enamel basin filled with warm water and Dettol. The water turned red and had to be emptied twice. She finally located the cut— "A tiny cut, really. But there's always so much blood from the head"—and closed the wound with a sticking plaster.

. . . you remember Grace who used to work upstairs for Mrs. Mainzer she's left now also the Harmon's girl left there's mainly young ones now they drink and go out with tsotsis they don't like me because I don't drink with them they poured water under my door. Why don't you come to our parties they ask, There a lot of rubbish they cut up my uniforms when I was out, make noise all night I can't sleep I have a headache the next day. . . .

Christmas. Africans shuffle along, singing, spitting as they yell filthy imprecations that make Mark and his younger brother giggle from their hiding place on the balcony. The doorbell rings constantly as Africans arrive to claim their "Christmas Box." They know his mother to be a soft touch, and Africans from as far away as the pharmacy in Rosebank somehow find themselves at the Spiegelmans' door. Years later Mark can always make his parents laugh with his imitation of an African his mother doesn't recognize demanding a present. "Hau, missis. I'm the boy for carry-it the groceries. Is me, Esteban, missis, for putting-it the food inna car. How you don't know me?"

Whenever I think of the kids I take out my Album and I have a look at the pictures I do miss you a lot but you are faraway I cant even come & visit, money's the problem. The Mainzers also went on a holiday they left the end of October. Its only the 2 of them at home here,

*Johnny lives in Isreal, Lenny is also still aboard its
only Roy who still lives here. Did I send you a recipe
of cabbage white and red with nuts? The family are all
well Lenora always asks after you she got a job at last.
She's by herself & the kids the husband left he's really
useless he drinks too much does not see to the kids she's
saving to get a divorce. Mam please when you write to
Joel give him my regards*

Tell Jeff I will write to him soon.

Love to all the family.

PS I will be visiting you someday

When they used to go to the seaside, Doreen would
ask the children to bring her back some ocean water in
a jar. When they asked her why, Doreen told them that
she liked to drink it. "It keeps her regular," Mrs. Spiegelman explained.

Mark would neglect to fill the empty mayonnaise jar
until the last day of the holiday, remembering it only
occasionally as he peered into the mesmerizing depths
of tidepools, butterfly net near at hand. The closing
ritual of the holiday was always that before-breakfast
dash down the cliffside past the narrow-gauge railway
to the beach. There he would take off his shoes and
wade knee-deep into the surf to fill the jar, being careful not to get too much sand along with the seawater.
Then Mark would climb slowly up the footpath back to
the hotel, pausing to dig his bare feet deep into the cool
red dust. When he held the jar to the sun he would see
tiny particles floating in the clear water, some of them
minute living creatures that propelled themselves to
and fro.

They went to the same hotel every year. The first
year, when Mark was seven and Joel five, was the only
time Doreen had gone away with them. The first few
days had been miserable, Mark and his brother having

to eat in the Children's Diningroom, which was crowded and noisy with squalling children barely contained by their African nannies who simply raised their voices to converse above the appalling din. Mr. Spiegelman talked to the Indian headwaiter who said the children could eat in the adult dining room provided they "behaved like grownups." It meant dressing properly for each meal: tight shirt collars and wet hair brushed hard down on sensitive scalps, but the rewards were real food and the affectionate admiration of the waiters. Bobbie, the Indian headwaiter, would come by at each meal, raise three fingers to his lips with a smacking sound, and say, "Good eating, yes?" while the children tried to suppress their giggles.

When they came home from holiday they would regale Doreen with the tales of their adventures. Mrs. Spiegelman would tell her how, when told that a favorite waiter had been fired because he drank, little Joel responded: "Well, maybe he was thirsty."

"I remember that boy," Doreen had laughed. "He used to always tell the children dirty stories."

Mark would tell her all about the multicolored fish he had seen in the tide pools and how he *almost* stepped on a brown mamba while walking on the river path.

"Why doesn't Doreen come with us? We miss her," he had asked his mother during their holiday. "Because sometimes Doreen likes to see her own family," his mother had replied.

Mark vaguely remembered meeting Doreen's daughter, Lenora. She was lanky and thin and bore little resemblance to her mother. In her arms she had carried a small child with a running nose, his head shaved against ringworm.

On his first return visit to South Africa, Mark stayed with his older sister, who lived in a Spanish-style house in the suburb of Melrose with her husband and two children. One Thursday, the two of them went to pick up Doreen on her "day off." Mark, now a gangly teenager, towered over Doreen. "Now we're really Mutt and Jeff, hey, Dor?" he said. Doreen seemed embarrassed and uneasy in his presence. She seemed even more so when they sat and had tea under his sister's pleasantly shaded veranda by the swimming pool. "Yes, missis. Thank you, missis," Doreen said to Eileen's offer of another biscuit with her tea. The ensuing silence was broken only by the sound of the birds thrashing among the branches of the mulberry tree. As far as Mark could remember, Doreen had always called his sister by the pet name he had given her: Dixie.

Mark told Doreen all about his job working on a bus survey for a market-research firm. Basically, the job consisted of standing on the street all day, stopping buses, and counting the number of people on each of the two decks. "When I got the job," he said, "they told me that if there are Coloureds on the back of the bus, I should count them as people."

"That's nice," Doreen said. She stood up and began to stack the dishes neatly on the tray.

"Leave it, Dor—" Dixie started to say, but her attention was distracted by her two-year-old, who was waddling toward them foaming at the mouth. She reached her fingers into his mouth and disgustedly pulled out a partially masticated garden snail, which she flicked into the bushes. The child began to wail with great heartbroken sobs, while Mark ineffectually tried to wash out its mouth with cold tea. "He's like you, Mutt," Doreen said happily. "You was always putting everything in your mouth."

Mark and Dixie took the tea things into the kitchen, Mark almost dropping the full tray as his eyes adjusted from the bright sunlight of the garden to the cool darkness of the house's interior. "Yuck, a snail," Dixie said as she ran hot water over the dishes in the sink. When they returned outside, Avi was sitting on Doreen's capacious lap staring at her with wondering eyes as she sang softly to him in Afrikaans.

While in college in the United States, Mark studies Modern Poetry with the thought that someday he would like to be a poet. The first poem he ever memorized was a ditty in "Kitchen Dutch" and was taught to him by Doreen. It goes like this:

> *Ouma en Oupa sit op die stoep,*
> *Oupa let off a helluva poep,*
> *Ouma sê: Wat makeer?*
> *Oupa sê: My mag is seer.*

This ditty about Oupa's stomach ailments resurfaces at inappropriate times in Mark's life—during an exam, in the middle of a serious conversation, while making love. For no reason at all, he will find himself waking up in the middle of the night chortling, *"My mag is seer."* (My stomach hurts.) He remembers how when he would come home tearful from a fall, knees badly scraped from crashing his bike in some daredevil game, Doreen would start him laughing by asking in Afrikaans what was wrong: *Wat makeer?*

> *...I have to wash doors, walls, do washing. the boy only does the stove, windows and sweep....I really enjoyed my holiday at Potch even though it was so hot. Here in Joburg it rain now & again even now its raining. Killarney is no more save, too many muggings, Robbery & Killings going on, nearly all the flats are & buildings are fenced with ~~boys~~ guards during the day & night they are busy here now.*

... tell Dixie I am happy she's well and about again.
I am earning R.90 now but things clothing, food is too
expensive plus tax. Hope the family Master you and
the Boys are all fine.

> *Good night*
> *Love to all the family*

Love also from the family.

Mark is watching television in his apartment in New
York City. On the news there is a brief feature on a
demonstration at the University of Cape Town. The
censors have been forced to temporarily let up, thanks
to a court order, and this is the first live footage in a
while. We see some students shouting slogans, march-
ing around with banners. Suddenly we see the police
firing tear gas, running forward. A young girl drops
her banner and starts to run. A policeman quickly
catches up with her and begins to beat her in that near-
comic slow motion of real violence. We see the whip
rise and fall, rise and fall. The girl is slim and blond.
She sits down, hugs herself as if she is cold. The policeman runs on. The scene changes to another riot in a
township. Small black children dart out from between
shacks and toss stones with the accuracy of champion
cricketers. Howzat! A policeman crumples to the
ground and is hustled into a truck. A spiderweb appears across the windshield of the photographers' van.
End of footage.

I dont know will I be able to move back to Potch
when I leave the Gillins the goverment says you are too
dark you have to live in the bantustan. I went to see
your friend Mr Bernstein you know the one whose a
lawyer his brother is in the same office. He said Doreen
its nonsense you can live there if you want they cant

*stop you. I don't know what it means I can live with
Lenora but she has the kids her place is too small....*

Mark goes to visit his former roommate, Saul, on
95th Street, where, coincidentally, another South African has moved into the room Mark vacated. "Give
these South African Jews a foothold and you can't get
rid of them," Saul joked.

"Hey, how's it?" Danny, the replacement South
African, says. "You've got to see this book. A friend
of mine at Ravan just sent it to me."

The book is a collection of drawings done by children
in Soweto. Like most children's drawings, these are
crude: stick figures, the perspective misjudged so that
people are larger than houses. And what are the children of Soweto drawing today? Look, this is a policeman shooting at your brother. Here are children crying
from tear gas. Here some children play with the nice
police dog. See how sharp his teeth are. Here is a policeman being "throwed on with stones." Here is a
Casspir armored vehicle in the schoolyard. Here is a
funeral. Here is a funeral. Here is a funeral.

Dearest Madam & fam.

*Thanks very much for the letter and contents which
is 20 rand thanks again it came in very handy I am
going to buy myself something very nice. The weather
is very hot its really boiling you can hardly sleep at
night. I had a lovely Xmas & a very happy New Year
only it was too short, I didn't see everybody I wanted
to see but I enjoyed it anyhow. I am alright now, you
know the doctor was wrong I havent got heart trouble
thats what the doctor said at the hospital he's a German. What I really have is high blood pressure I go to
the hospital once a month for tablets. I am happy that
you are nearer to Dixie. The kids must be big. Eden*

Mews the Mews, Gardens are all sold out only some of the old tenants move out, but nearly everyone bought his own flat. I am happy that you're all still well especially Master....

Mark's sister, Dixie, also lives in San Diego now. Mark is visiting her when some other South Africans come over to spend the afternoon. One who is just visiting the area is Beryl, Dixie's childhood friend, who has children the same age as her own. Beryl is slim and attractive, though her skin is a little dry and taut across her face and lines crinkle outward from the corners of her eyes, the legacy of years of playing tennis in the sun. Avi, who is now nine, always liked Beryl's maid, and he asks: "How is Selma?"

"I've got another Selma now," Beryl replies, turning to arrange food on a tray. Mark winks at his nephew who is looking nonplussed and twists his index finger in the direction of his forehead. The child grins, understanding now.

Mark joins his parents out on the veranda where they are telling his brother-in-law, Arthur, about Doreen.

"I don't know," Arthur muses. "I'd hate to think people assumed I was dead every time I haven't written to them for a while. Maybe she just got tired of writing to her old master and missis. Maybe her daughter told her to stop. Lots of things could have happened."

His parents are indignant at this idea. After all, they have been corresponding with her for almost twenty years and this is the first time she has failed to send a Christmas card or acknowledge the money they have sent her. "And besides," his mother says, "we sent her a fair amount of money every year. I'm sure it came in very handy. How can we go on sending her money if she doesn't write back to us?"

...Master must be happy with the swimming pool as he likes to swim you know that old lady at Eden Mansions remember the one who looks like she's got a hunch I dont know if shes German or Hollander she always talked to you at the swimming pool she died 2 weeks back the husband died a year ago. Love to Dixie and the family....

There is quite a community of South Africans living in this part of Southern California. In the manner of immigrants everywhere, all it takes is a couple of families to establish a foothold for others to quickly follow. And then, the weather is almost identical to that of Johannesburg, allowing for a lifestyle in which swimming and tennis-playing feature prominently. Dixie invites Mark to a "citizenship party" held at the home of one such resident, Beryl's sister, Shareen.

"You've never been to the Stillmans' place, have you?" Dixie asks. "Well, there'll be a little surprise for you there."

The surprise turns out to be that the Stillmans have brought their coloured servant Sofi with them to America. Sitting on the attractive outdoor patio with its swimming pool and view of a sagebrush- and scrub-filled canyon, Mark watches Sofi move among the guests with a tray of hors d'oeuvres. "It's *déjà vu* all over again," he says to his father. As if on cue, the hostess calls out: "Sofi, my girl, just bring me one of those cold drinks, quick now."

Mark wonders where Sofi stays. Does she have a little room to herself in the house or are there some servants' quarters on the grounds? Does she perhaps live in the Mexican neighborhood and ride a bus to her missis' house?

He remembers how he and Lenny had once gone over to the servants' quarters in The Mews, the oldest section of flats in the Eden complex. They had noticed an

open window in one of the rooms and had climbed up
the drainpipe to peer inside. The interior of the servant's room was disappointing; it smelled musty and
stale and there was no mystery to the cramped space
with its iron bedstead, humble bedside table and ancient radio. Their expedition was not a complete failure, though. A maid from The Mews spotted them and
she chased them several hundred yards, swatting at
them with a rolled-up magazine and calling them cockroaches.

Mark finds himself in conversation with a pasty-
faced South African girl of about his own age who
works in advertising. She tells him she is not really
worried about events in South Africa.

"You see, my parents have a flat in London. So if
things get really bad they can always move there." She
confides that she herself left because "you just can't
make money there anymore." Luckily the host is calling everybody to gather around him, and Mark is able
to extricate himself from having to make further polite
conversation. The party is in honor of the fact that the
Stillmans have just been granted U.S. citizenship, and
now an enormous three-tier cake in the colors of the
American flag is brought out. The guests' doubts as to
whether to salute the cake or eat it is quickly dispelled
by the host carving triangular shaped wedges in it with
a large knife. Mark takes a piece of what turns out to
be mainly vanilla ice cream and goes to sit with his
mother, who is deep in conversation with Sofi.

"I'm saving money so's I can buy one of those little
houses in Dube," Sofi is saying. "But it's lonely here,
missis. I wish I could leave tomorrow."

Later, Sofi shows Lena Spiegelman some black-and-
white snapshots of her grandchildren. Mark glances
over their shoulders to get a glimpse of a tall, thin
African child looking shyly to the right of the camera,

his hand resting on his smaller brother's shoulder. "And this one must be Vusi?" his mother is saying while Sofi beams with pleasure.

Mark's father is amused. The previous night he and his wife had argued for a long time over the fact that a friend of theirs was extremely upset that her son had married a Zulu woman. Charles had remarked that the woman was just being prejudiced; as long as the son's wife was a decent person, what did it matter what color she was? Mark's mother had disagreed. She felt that there were always problems when people of different backgrounds married.

"You know," Charles says now, "your mother is the only person I know who can spend the afternoon talking to the maid without making it seem like condescension.

"I think she can get away with it," he adds, after some thought, "because she's really not a liberal."

Dearest Mam & Master,

I hope this letter to find you in good health. Wishing you a very happy ~~Pasach~~ holiday over the week and a happy Easter. Sorry for having delayed so long to write and say thanks for what you are doing for me. Its because I have been in hospital for 3 weeks I went for a check up and they kept me there saying my high blood was too low they kept me from the 27 March I only got discharged on Saturday 14th April They gave me tablets for my high blood. I was alright all of a sudden the nurses gave me different tablets till I left. They gave the right ones and the other 2 kinds which they gave me there which I dont know I know which is the right ones, on arriving home they phoned I must throw the other 2 pks away as they are the wrong ones. I went to hosp. again I went to the physiartricist yesterday I still do not feel right. I only hope for the best.

Please thank Joel, Mark, Master not forgetting your-
self for everything you are doing for me. Mrs Gillin
got me the money from the Standard Bank. Thanks
also to master for the note he enclosed for me. When
phoning to Dixie, Joel give them my regards....

Mark's parents are told about a low-priced package
tour and they make their first trip back to South Africa
in fifteen years. On their first night back in the States,
Mark talks to them on the telephone. They sound
hoarse and exhausted; the tour was "an absolute whirl-
wind, no time to even catch our breath," they tell him.

"I'd forgotten how beautiful the country is," his
father says. "And we saw the most magnificent game
at Kruger. You would have loved it."

"We went back to Eden Gardens," his mother
chimes in from another extension. "It was very different, everything was locked up and you had to ring a
bell at the main entrance just to get in. So we rang the
bell and this huge African with a bald head opened it
and says: 'What do you want?' Then he looks at us and
yells 'One-Oh-Five,' and he throws his arms around
your father."

"It was Suleiman," Mr. Spiegelman says. This was
the day watchman who used to shout at Mark for riding a bicycle in the parking garage, back when they
lived in 105 Eden Gardens. "Oh, he was so happy to
see us. He kept asking 'How's Mark? How's Joel?' It
was quite touching."

"I asked him about Doreen," Mark's mother adds.
"He also thought she must have died. He said she went
funny in the head toward the end, but I'm not sure I
believe him. Suleiman was always such a liar."

... Winter is closing in we only get rain now some
days its hot some days cold The kids are wearing jer-

seys to school already coming home tying them around their waists. They are all keeping well. I am going to buy myself warm underwear and a coat with my present you know I am always cold in winter although I like winter because in summer I always get those hot flashes.

Thank you for all you are doing for me love to master not forgetting yourself tell Mutt to not be so lazy and write the money was R.89.60.

Love Dor.

THE UGLY BEETLE

"Ohhh, ugly one! You are uglier than the grasshopper in its change of life. You are too ugly to live." Danger Mololofo, brother to the hyena, the broken one, the too-too-ugly, the *toktokkie* beetle, stood before the plate-glass window and stared at his image. He reached into the cavernous World War II trench coat that had once belonged to his father, and drew out an old cartridge case filled with snuff. Digging into it with one hard horny nail, he pulled out a tiny shovelful of snuff. This he placed carefully in his right nostril. From the left nostril—that little slit in a misshapen mound of flesh —he pulled a ... toktokkie beetle. How the image in the window laughed! Some snuff fell onto his thick, broken upper lip, but with a quick "whoo" and a snuffle he had inhaled it again. He sneezed and laughed once more. It was a pity that the Sotho dustbin boys

were too wary of him to come and laugh at his little
act. They only ran by him with their loaded dustbins,
afraid to look into his face. And it was much too early
in the morning for any whites to be out on the street
and pass him with a look of disgust and a muttered
"Kaffir beggar." Ahh, they all feared him. Even the
police were afraid to touch him. He smelled too bad!
Again he and his mirror twin chuckled at their shared
joke.

But this was a good place for him. There was no
blackness in his heart today. It was here that he had
seen how to use his powers in the city. He had just
come to the golden city, Egoli, and was walking the
sun-drenched streets in this very same coat. His eye
had been caught by the reflection in the shop window.
It was the first time he had ever seen and examined his
full-length image, and he looked upon the picture with
self-hatred. No wonder the villagers had shunned him.
No wonder they had feared him, and, afraid to say
anything to him, had called the half-tame stray hyena
that hung around the village by his own name. No wonder the young girls hid their faces and giggled when
he passed.

It was not his fault that he was ugly, that his face
was twisted and broken, that his hips bulged, that his
back hunched around his wide shoulders. He had been
born a twin, and, as was customary, he and his brother
had been placed in the middle of the cattle path leading
back into the kraal. The cows' hooves were to decide
which of them was to live. His brother had been the
lucky one and had been killed outright. But where he
lay it was muddy and the cow that rested its hoof on
his face had decided to shift its weight at the last moment. He had survived, but the hoofmark was still
there . . . as it would be until he once again lay in the
mud. His father had wanted him strangled and buried

with his smashed and dead brother. His mother had
said nothing; it was not her place to say anything, and
anyway, she still had an older child to suckle. He owed
his life to his grandmother, who took it upon herself to
bring him up. She had told the others that those who
disobeyed the directives of the Great Spirit as shown
by His servants the cows would surely be punished. She
also told them that anyone who bore the mark of the
cattle's favor would surely become a great witch doctor, an *iNyanga* among iNyangas. Ah, but the old
witch, the sorceress-whom-no-one-dared-accuse had
gone against tradition herself. She should have named
him Cattlespared, or Kinefavored, as surviving twins
are always called. But no, she had named him Vouyo
after her husband, the famous warrior who had fought
at the battle of Isandlhwana, who had taken part in the
slaughter of a whole British garrison. How she must
have hated the old warrior who had married her as an
old man and had deserted her, pregnant with his child,
to go off no one knew where. How she must have hated
him to name this misshapen, disfigured infant after the
great warrior.

He knew what she was about, had always known
what she was about, and had taken it upon himself to
hate her. She did not want a great iNyanga. She
wanted a half-wit servant who would do her bidding,
would make her medicines more potent, more valuable,
with his cattle-favored touch. He had even heard it
whispered in the village that it was she, not the long lie
in the wet mud as an infant, who had twisted his body
until even the crookbacked hyena seemed whole com-
pared to him.

But that cow's blow on the head did not make him
stupid. He had shown the old woman. At first, when he
was very small, he had followed her around, hopping
like a little toad and putting up with her slaps and

constant grumbling. As soon as he was old enough to
be aware of himself, he knew what her purpose was. He
remembered everything that she told him, sorting it
out until he knew her hidden motives. He learned to
run off into the veld, leaving undone the tasks she had
set him. Let the old witch fill her own bucket from the
river . . . if she could find where he had discarded the
bucket. Let her watch the porridge on the fire; that was
woman's work. And if it burned and stuck to the iron
cooking pot, so much the better. He could always find
food at other huts. He would appear at their doors like
a malevolent spirit blown in from the veld, making the
villagers afraid not to feed him.

Unlike the other villagers, who never ventured into
it alone and rarely at night, he loved the veld. He
would lie in the dust in the warm sunlight watching
the lizards and the insects running back and forth from
grass stalk to grass stalk, from stone to stone. He was
not afraid of the snakes or poisonous scorpions, not
even of the ten-inch *songololos,* with their thousand
legs, that curled into a little wheel when he picked them
up. Even the old witch shuddered at the sight of them.
But not he.

He started spending most of his time out on the veld
after the Thing had come over him for the first time.
His grandmother had told him soon after he learned to
talk, how a Thing would take over his mind, revealing
him to be a great witch doctor. She told him that when
the Thing came on him, his talk would make barren
women fertile, would reveal the hiding places of stolen
goods, would sniff out witches. She would take note of
all he said, and together they would hold sway over the
whole district. She even tried to hasten Its arrival by
feeding him strange soups and powders. She would
wake him at the peak of the full moon to go out and
gather herbs on the veld. She would never touch these

herbs, but would have him pick them and put them into a bag for her. Then, one day, as he was sitting by the fire waiting for the evening porridge, he felt his jaws clamp shut and a great darkness shut out his sight. When he opened his eyes again, his grandmother was towering over him, her hate-filled eyes boring into him. "You lay there like a toktokkie beetle playing dead," she hissed. "You didn't move. You didn't speak. The spirit that came into you was a dead one." With that, she shot a wad of spittle full into his face. He did not stop hating her from then on.

The following day he had woken at sunrise and rushed straight out into the veld. He found a little ebony toktokkie beetle at the very first place he stopped. He tapped it on its bent, horny back. Its legs stiffened, and it lay rigid as if it had been dead for years and had dried up in this shape. He lifted it carefully and placed it on a flat rock. Still it did not stir. Grasping another rock, he smashed the beetle again and again until there was nothing left but pulp. Then he lay weeping among the stones and thorns and dust until the Thing came, splaying his crooked body as rigid as the beetle's had been. When he recovered, he knew he would never injure a toktokkie again.

The half-grown hyena that was always on the outskirts of the village and that was named after him began to follow him out into the veld. He would occasionally throw it some choice insect—a fat locust, a succulent caterpillar—which the animal would snap down greedily. He soon learned to imitate its high whooping cry that tapered into a mad cackle, learned it well enough to set all the dogs in the village barking whenever he chose.

One day, a group of herd boys crept up on him and the animal as he was throwing it fat maggots he had found under a rock. The herd boys surrounded the

hyena and set to beating it with the long sticks they
carried to prod the cattle. The animal rushed madly
around in a circle, trying to escape from its tormentors.
With an angry moan, he had rushed forward at the
largest of the herd boys, twisted the stick away, and,
seizing the other youth in his crooked hands, tossed him
several feet away into a thornbush. The hyena dashed
off, its loping gait carrying it quickly out of sight. He
stood, waiting impassively for any retribution the herd
boys might visit upon him. They stared at him, then
slunk away one by one. They had been taught to fear
his ugliness. Now, looking anew at the cowlike boss on
his back, they feared his strength as well. Some days
later, the hyena disappeared. He eventually came upon
its carcass dangling from a crude wire snare. The animal had struggled for a long time, and the wire had
cut so deep it could barely be seen.

Still, he stayed in the village. Even when his age-
mates had all left to seek work in the mines and the
cows were followed by successive new groups of herd
boys, he stayed. He slept more and more often on the
veld, spending days in a row there, eating flying ants,
locusts, marula plums, and wild figs. He and the old
woman barely looked at each other, although he would
now and then bring her herbs and insects as she was
becoming too feeble to hunt for them herself. One night
he came into the hut to find her stretched across a pile
of her medicines. She was as stiff as he became when
the Thing was on him. He felt his eyes rolling upward
but managed to control them until the blackness passed
and he could see clearly again. It was the first time he
had mastered the Thing. He knew that he had to leave
right then. If he stayed in the hut, he would never be
free from the old witch's influence. He lifted the old
woman's light body, the smell of death attacking his
nostrils, and laid her down on the straw pallet where

she normally slept. For a moment he considered burying her, but then the villagers would think that he had done away with her.

He looked around the small hut. Everything in it was familiar to him, even the medicines stacked in the corner. He had never been allowed to touch them except when she directed him, but the old woman had shown him the uses of all her stock. He knew how to throw the talking bones to see the future or the past, which herbs or amulets were for barrenness, for pain, for unhappy lovers. He rolled all of the medicines in a blanket and then dropped them into a large flour bag, all the time expecting the old woman to leap on him with slaps and curses. But the dead woman did not stir. It took him only a few minutes to gather everything he wanted, and then he was out of the hut forever.

It was a moonlit night and he had no trouble finding his way across the veld. By daybreak he had reached the road he and his grandmother had always taken to the monthly market. To the left lay the small market town; to the right, far, far in the distance, was the golden city. Without hesitating, he turned right.

He traveled down the road for a number of days, walking until he was given a ride by one of the fruit-and-vegetable wagons headed for the city. Then, when he was almost at the city's outskirts, he stopped. He no longer felt drawn to it. Instead, he walked into a collection of buildings surrounded by a high fence. He walked until he saw a man leaning with his back against one of the buildings. The man looked at him and said, ''Yes, you'll do. You're ugly enough to scare anybody.'' He was not surprised that the man spoke to him in his own tongue, instead of in the apes' gibberings he had heard on the road. He had felt this place to be a good one for him.

He worked as a night watchman until the summer

had passed and come again. Although he hardly spoke to anyone, he listened carefully until their strange yammering had settled into words he could understand. During this time, he lived in a crowded collection of tin huts; yet his life was as solitary as it had been in the village. He would often hear the sound of men's and women's laughter intermingled, and would grow angry and jealous. But he knew that it would be no good approaching any woman, ugly as he was. Still, he wanted one. At the laughingly given suggestion of the bossboy who had hired him, he went to visit a whore. Following the bossboy's directions, he came to a cluster of huts reeking of homemade beer. A number of women were sitting around a small fire. When he stepped into the firelit circle, they all laughed. He heard one say, "Ugh. Who would want to lie with that ugly beetle?" Another woman said, "Let's give him Esther," and again they all laughed, slapping their thighs in merriment.

Esther proved to be thin. When she spoke she gave a dry, rattling cough that told him of the nearness of her death. He looked once with longing at a woman with tremendous thighs who sat close to the fire swilling beer out of a tin pail. She would surely buck like a mare in full heat! Then he followed Esther into the hut. She pulled off her cheap coverall and lay down on a heap of flour bags and blankets, her eyes shut. In his excitement, he did not bother to undress fully, throwing himself upon her with such force that she gave a loud groan of pain. When he had finished, she suddenly turned her head aside and vomited. He could smell blood, beer, and vomit; his arm was sticky, his loins and spirit drained. He drew back his fist to strike her, but stopped himself in time. How easy it would be to kill a stick like that.

He was already out of the hut when her retching

started again. The handsome fat woman was standing outside, a thin smile playing on her lips. He paid her what she asked. Two weeks pay for that, when a flour sack would have done just as well. "I hope you didn't kill her, O thou cockroach," the fat woman called to him as he walked off into the darkness. A curse on her and all her tribe!

Yes, he was best off by himself. His real happiness was when he was alone at night, armed with a long hardwood stick, his feet warmed by the charcoal brazier that gave off a soft glow barely penetrating the pitch-dark nights. He would bring with him a small sack full of toktokkie beetles that he had captured and tamed. He would put them one by one onto the ground and watch them stagger off into the surrounding dark. Some while later, he would take out his snuff box, lay it carefully on the ground and lightly—oh, so lightly —tap it with the long hard nail of his forefinger. A few minutes later he would tap it again, his ear keen to the soft answering taps from the darkness. This was how the toktokkie's wife called him to her, but he had trained them to come back to his tapping only. Eventually, the beetles would come staggering into the firelight, one by one, until they were all safely deposited back in their bag. Heh! Those beetles! Their shells were hard, yet how easy it was for a man to crush them if he wanted to. But they would faithfully return to him from who knows what distances, through the many hazards that beset such a small creature, all for a tapping so soft that no man could hear it.

The time came when he could no longer ignore the call of the city. Instead of going to his usual place to stand watch, he packed up his beetles and herbs and, unnoticed by anyone, walked out of the compound. By daybreak he was in the middle of the golden city itself. But that was all. No further call came to him, not even the whispered suggestion of a direction. For the first

time in his life he did not know who he was, where he
was. He stumbled along the clean-swept, hard streets
for hours, wondering how he would surmount all this
brightness and glitter. He was near fainting from the
heat. He, who could lie all day on a slab of hot rock in
the veld, outlasting even the lizards. He feared that the
beetles would die, suffocated in their sweltering sack.
But this was foolishness.

Then, catching his reflection in a shop window, he
walked toward it. He watched his ugliness for a long
time, moving closer and closer to his reflected image
until his shadow finally obscured it and he could look
into the shop itself. A tall white man was drinking
water from a bubble of glass. Without thinking, he
pushed open the door and walked in. "Give me water,"
he said, pointing at the bubble. The white man stared
at him, open-mouthed with astonishment and anger,
then called: "Samson! Get this stinking Kaffir out of
here." A black man came out of one of the blurry
shadows in the back of the shop and started toward
him. Then the Thing came. He had not thought of it
since his grandmother's death and It had left him
alone. Now he could feel It pulling him into a blackness
deeper and darker than the burrow of an ant-bear. His
eyes rushed skyward; only the whites were showing.
He stood, swaying slightly, feeling himself returning
as if from a great journey. Samson's voice range in his
ears, "I not touch him. He is danger." He was back!
He could see Samson trembling with fear, watching
him with widened eyes, ants' eggs of sweat breaking on
his forehead. The white man cursed at them both and,
with a grimace of disgust, started leading him out of
the shop. "Danger." It was a good name. He went
along docilely, laughing to himself at the white fool
not knowing how easy it was for him to break the back
of an ordinary, upright man.

. . .

Like the silver ball on a gambling wheel, his memory
had at last rolled back to the nought. The images of the
past faded, and he was left again with his own image
grinning idiotically at him. He turned away from the
window, walked a few paces and sat down with his back
against the wall. He took out his begging cup, dropped
a few small coins into it and set it down beside him. He
had learned much since the day that he had walked
into the shop. And yet it had all come to him in the
moment he had heard his new name and pulled himself
back from the Thing. All confusion had left him by the
time he was escorted out of the shop. The sun did not
oppress him. He studied the city as he would a rock
turned over to expose the creatures hiding under it,
and now he knew it as well as he had ever known the
veld. This was made easy by being a beggar, for he
traveled where he pleased. The police had stopped him
a few times, but each time he would act as if the Thing
had come over him and they would leave him alone,
occasionally giving his rigid body a few kicks but soon
stopping for fear of soiling their shiny black boots. He
also earned more than he had as a night watchman, his
ugliness earning coins for him. But money was of little
concern to him. Why, he could earn all he wished by
selling amulets to the *tsotsis* to give them good luck in
dice or the gambling wheel, or to protect them from
injuries in their gang wars. Even the tsotsis, who con-
trolled the township with their violence and money
schemes, recognized him as an iNyanga. Ah, but he had
angered them . . . for he refused to waste his powers on
silly amulets that he did not believe in. He did not want
to barter so crudely for gain, and, besides, he knew that
his powers worked only when he followed their call.
    If he could bring the tsotsis under his control by
rolling his eyes, instead of merely putting some fear
into them, he could surely do anything he wanted to

with the city. If the tsotsis would take their guidance from him, he could pull the city along an invisible string as surely as he had drawn the toktokkie beetles out of the darkness with his tapping. It would be so easy. It only needed a man beside a brazier to accomplish everything, and he was such a man. He knew everything about the city and could go anywhere, where the thieves would run into trouble with the police. He listened to the children talking about their holidays, and knew which houses would be deserted and for how long. He knew which night watchmen liked to drink or to smoke *dagga* and other potent herbs, which had girlfriends, which had the greatest fear of spirits. He knew how to get around them all, by his powers as well as by his observation. He knew how to cause problems with the simplest of tricks.

One evening he had been walking down a quiet side street, when he spied a man and a woman about to eat their dinner in the servants' quarters of a large house. It was a warm night, the door was open and he could see everything in the little room. He found himself walking up the driveway and into the room. "Quick," he said. "The boss wants his table right now." He handed the lamp from the table to the astonished maidservant, gave the food-laden dishes to her man friend, and disappeared down the driveway with the table on his back. Several blocks away he had thrown the little table into some nearby bushes and roared with laughter. How long would those fools stand there holding their lamps and dishes before asking "the boss" why he needed the table? Would they realize that they had been fooled, or would they just think it was more of the white man's craziness?

If he could only get the tsotsis to listen to him, to stop their aimless stealing and killing in the township but play mystical tricks on the city, why, he could turn the whole city topsy-turvy as he did with the flat rocks on the veld. And just as the termites and colorless maggots under the rocks perished in the hot sun, so would the pale-fleshed inhabitants of the city squirm and die!

But he had had trouble with the tsotsis, and not only over the amulets he would not sell them. A few days before, he had returned to the small room in the township where he usually slept. Before he reached the little shack, he had the feeling that there were people inside, so he was not surprised to find three tsotsis from the Russian Gang standing in the middle of the room. They had not touched anything, fearing the curses an iNyanga lays on meddlers with his property. Nevertheless, the youths looked him boldly in the face. He widened his eyes, which made them look away. But then one of them arrogantly spoke to him, "Hey, man. Us olds was thinking like what you got them beetles an' things so what you say we make toktokkie races an' has the gambling blokes come blow their wads?" It was more a statement than a question, but he surprised them by answering in their own patois. "You want I be in race too? Look, I be beetle." And with that he hopped a step forward, driving them against the wall. He held out his open hand, turned it around and made a fist, turned it again, and opened it with a toktokkie nestling in the center of his palm. "It be easy do you know where they hide," he said, motioning the gang members out the door with his other hand. Two of them hurried out into the darkness, but the leader stopped at the doorstep. He reached beneath the blanket he wore wrapped around him and pulled out a long knife. He waved it over his head. "We're the Russians," he said, and then moved quickly away.

Some time before, walking down the alleys late at night, he had sensed danger behind him. He had turned quickly and the club aimed at his head had whooshed past, lightly grazing his shoulder. He knocked the club away with one hand, grabbed the man's throat with the other. He pulled the man's face right up to his own, then crushed his assailant's windpipe with a single powerful squeeze, sucking the dying man's last breath with his open mouth. It was said that if you breathe another's last gasp, his soul would be your servant forever. But was this really true? Perhaps the man was also a Russian and the gang had by now guessed who had killed him in such a strange fashion. One morning, he had passed a bloody body lying in a gutter. He knew that even an iNyanga could be killed by bullets. But he was not afraid. He would surely smell death before it came, and he smelled nothing now. Good, tonight he would go talk to the Russians. He would not worry about his beetles, for the gang would become his beetles. He would tell them his plans and offer to be their "brains." They would either listen to him, or, insulted, they would kill him. But he did not smell death!

He started at the sudden loud *chunk* of coins in his beggar's cup. A tall white woman, her lips sharply painted red, was looking down at him.

"Oh, you poor man," she said.

THANK GOD FOR INFORMERS

Once you get hold of someone like Lennox Sibiza you can't let him go. And if his wife or his mistress or daughter comes to ask for his old cap or overcoat, you have to tell her: No, it's State Property now. Nothing. Not a button or a shoelace, a half-smoked cigarette. If it belonged to him, lock it in the deepest, most hidden vault and post a twenty-four-hour guard. You never know what subversion can be made out of the most innocent object.

I have told Chief of Police Krieger this on many occasions, and he has always listened to me with a sympathetic ear and the promise to pass my words on to Government House. But the politicians always know better than a humble policeman, and so they make mistakes. If they would learn from their mistakes, that at least would be something. Then, perhaps, they would pay heed to us little men who toil on the front lines to

keep them sleeping safe in their designer sheets and
their hillside mansions.

Sibiza's very first brush with the law—when he was
just a squeaking pip in the lowest ranks of the Azanian
Congress—should have been fair warning of what we
might expect from him. We had the goods on him:
photographs, names, dates, the lot ... even a cellmate's
confession that Sibiza had tried to talk him into stag-
ing a breakout. We underestimated the man and he
made a mockery of what should have been a show trial,
a warning to saboteurs and troublemakers everywhere.
First the defendant's lawyer got our detective to swear
he has seen Sibiza attending illegal meetings on a certain date in Johannesburg, then the lawyer produced a
newspaper photograph of Sibiza taken in Cape Town
on the very same day. The cache of illegal weapons
"found" in Sibiza's backyard was similarly proven to
have been in police hands several months before the
alleged discovery. Then there was Ndooli, who shared
Sibiza's cell at Leeuwkop. . . .

First a word about our friend Ndooli. Here was a
man so terrified of pain that there was no need to torture him, he did it to himself. The interrogating offi-
cers used to amuse themselves by placing various
innocent objects on the desk—a spanner, a pair of
pliers, a sewing kit—before having Ndooli brought in
to the office. There was no problem persuading him to
testify against Sibiza; as Hijndrijk said, he was ready
to swear Karl Marx was his grandmother. Ndooli said
all the words he had been coached to speak, but he
could not abide the defendant's steady stare and he
convinced no one with his hastily muttered disserta-
tion. As Ndooli was led away from the dock, Sibiza's
voice, so quiet and yet so distinct, could be heard
throughout the courtroom: "You ought to be ashamed
of yourself."

As soon as he was released, Ndooli wrote to all the

papers to say that his testimony was a lie, that he had
been forced into it by the police. We picked him up
immediately, of course, but the man we brought back
to the jail was not the same one who had left. It reminds me of the time I saw a hypnotist performing in
the assembly hall in Potchefstroom. He handed a hypnotized volunteer an onion and told him it was an
apple. The man ate it. He called the man's wife to the
stage and gave her a hatpin: "Stick it in his arse," the
hypnotist said. "Go on, give him a good poke." The
wife did as she was asked—not without enthusiasm,
mind you—but the bewitched fellow just grinned. He
didn't feel a thing. It was like that with Ndooli. The
same man who before trembled at the merest apprehen-
sion of a blow was now fearless. Hijndrijk, whose
professional pride was hurt by Ndooli's defection, almost killed him cranking up the current on the "wire-
less" just to get the satisfaction of a murmur or a
grunt.

Although I was familiar with his case, I didn't meet
Lennox Sibiza until the next time he was picked up, a
full year after the famous trial that ended in farce. It
should have been a routine interrogation, but somehow
everything was just that little bit off. I had the warder
lead him in while I was still reading his file, knowing
that it often unnerved prisoners to see me read their
life story while they sat waiting for the questions to
begin. There was a surprise in store for me, though;
something I had not noticed the first time I read his
file. There, under his name, was my exact birth date!
Perhaps this was what set me off balance—this and the
fact that we had grown up in the same small district of
Natal.

Sibiza didn't start talking just to break the silence,
as so many other prisoners would have done. I could
feel his inquiring gaze on me as I read and when I
eventually looked up he did not drop his eyes or try to

stare me down. It wasn't even as if he were taking my measure, but as if he knew it already. I held the paper out to him, but his eyes remained steady. He had no interest in finding out what was in his file.

"Look," I said. "We're born on the same day, in the same year, in the same place. What do you think of that? We could be twins." Sibiza did not respond. "What do you think it means, kaffir? Do you think we're brothers?"

To my astonishment, he laughed. It was a laugh of genuine amusement, a deep-throated chuckle. Didn't he know I could smash those articulate fingers with a hammer, that I could wire him up like an old battery to be recharged, could hang him upside down for days on end if I chose? Although I generally forswore such primitive methods, I had the full authority of the State to "use whatever means is necessary" to make him cooperate. I was not used to prisoners laughing at their interrogation.

"Brothers," he repeated, still chuckling. "I suppose we are."

When this unsatisfactory interview was over, I read through his file again with more care. It held no secrets, no hidden key to his personality. His life followed the standard pattern of so many who find themselves here : the boy who does well at the Mission School, who gets a scholarship to a boarding school in Swaziland, then it's on to Fort Hare University and the law degree. Those do-gooders who try to force education on the African never see where this path inevitably leads. You separate them from their tribal traditions, you let them think they're just as good as the white boss, and they get bitter at the things that are not open to them. My father had a saying : Let a monkey sit at the dinner table with you and the next thing you know he'll want to drive your car.

I'm not so sure we can blame Sibiza on any pattern,

though. I think he would have been dangerous even if
he had never learned to read and write. He had the gift
of always seeming to be in control, no matter how pow-
erless he really was.

I have to admit that our first meeting impressed me,
and I decided to keep my eye on him. I made sure to be
watching the next day as he and a group of prisoners
were led out into the exercise yard which, in those days,
was presided over by a giant from the Free State
named Ouks. Ouks was the kind of man who could form
an entire rugby scrum line by himself; he had been
brought up on a drought-stricken rural farm and he
had no patience with city Africans. I've seen many a
political *bandiet* learn to get a move on after a good
kick in the pants from Ouks. I watched Sibiza detach
himself from the group of prisoners who were doing a
smart jog trot around the open yard and walk at un-
ruffled pace over to the giant guard.

"Now you're for it, my boy," I said to myself, waiting for him to be pummeled into order. But what's
this? Sibiza is talking to Ouks, who shrugs his shoulders and seems undecided what to do next. The line of
hop-skipping Africans wavers, stops, breaks apart.
Now they are standing about in small groups, talking
to each other. Some have magically produced cigarettes
and are cheerfully puffing away. A few have gathered
around Sibiza and are listening while he holds forth as
if he is presiding over some tribal court.

Of course, Sibiza took his knocks. Not every Ouks
stayed his hand, but the men would get this strange
thoughtful look afterward, as if they had spat on a
national monument. And then, Sibiza knew how to
make an opportunity out of everything. I'm thinking
of how he got his lip split by Laggenkop on the very
day that stupid woman from Parliament was making a
surprise inspection of the jail. It wasn't long afterward

that an order came down from the Minister of Police himself to treat the man with restraint and special care.

No concession was enough for Sibiza. We could have set him up in a hotel and he would have organized room service to strike for better working conditions. He was inordinately clever about getting messages to the outside world, even from the remoteness of the Island: an innocent letter to his daughter on her fourth birthday would be passed by the prison censor, and practically the next day *that woman* would be telling Parliament: "Warder so-and-so struck prisoner such-and-such on this date; prisoner X has been denied his diabetes medicine; Sibiza has been refused access to books and note-paper." We would stop one conduit for information—his doctor, who visited him once a month from the mainland, for example—and another would already have been set up.

For years there were calls to release him, and not just from interfering foreigners and the liberal press but, more recently, from misguided elements in our own people. That so-very-clever young minister—you know the one, Van Rijnsberg, with the penciled-in mustache like some 1940s film star—and his "Sibiza is much more dangerous as a symbol of enchained leadership than he would be stalking up and down the country saying anything he damn well pleased." I think Van Rijnsberg and his lot envisaged Sibiza going quietly out to pasturage in the homelands to raise cattle and grandchildren.

I had hoped the pols would have learned from the second time they underestimated the man. This was when they let him out on bail during the sabotage trial, overconfident that someone so well known would not even dream of trying to elude "the world's most sophisticated secret police." Sibiza lost his tail within fifteen minutes of leaving the police station. The electronic pen planted in his release suit was never found, although hours later it was still transmitting strongly from the large rubbish dump thirty miles outside the city. How he managed to stay free for *months* still infuriates that generation of Special Service men whose promotions went up in smoke with each sighting of Sibiza ''concealed'' in the backseat of a tiny Hillman—one foot dangling out of the passenger window (he was a big man) as the car careened through the exclusive streets of Parktown North—and who each time arrived in force but five minutes too late to the Congress of Africa meetings that he had just finished addressing. Thank God for informers or he would still be out there today, mocking us.

It was after he was finally caught, tried, and convicted in spite of all the clever tricks of his little Jew lawyer, that my true acquaintance with him began. Think of the book I could write about him! I, who know the man so much better than any of those liberal journalists who have made themselves rich on his name and his story. After all, I have everything he said on tape.

I took a special interest in the case of Bantu Sibiza. Sometimes I followed his prison career from behind the scenes; but more and more, I was the one chosen to question him, to try to get him to see the light. I wonder sometimes whether this is anything to be proud of, for little he said was of any use to us. I realized early on— and with much irritation—that our sessions amused Sibiza, the battle of wits providing him with a pleasant distraction from his deluded thoughts about how he would lead the country in the future. Nevertheless, I decided to continue my debates with this strange prisoner, figuring that no man can forever avoid making a slip and that sooner or later I would find the hole in his armor. I even came to enjoy myself, as well. The

interrogation of an intelligent man is like a bout of
sumo wrestling—you have to watch your opponent
carefully, striking the instant you detect the slightest
weakening of will or equilibrium. Of course, the advantage is always on the side of the policeman, for he has
charge of the other's body and in the physical self is
the key to the mental. With that very rare exception.

Why was Sibiza the exception? I think it's because
he did not resist the degradation of imprisonment, the
daily wearing down that tells the incarcerated: You
are a thing, not a man. He simply did not notice it, did
not acknowledge the walls that surrounded him. For
all his intelligence, there was something wrong with
Sibiza's brain. He could not accept a reality different
from the one he carried around in his head. This is
what made the man dangerous. He had the vision of
the insane and was capable of infecting those around
him with it—which is why we took to frequently
changing the guards who kept watch on him.

With prisoners there is always something that becomes their way of keeping attached to this world. It
can be a certain way a midmorning shaft of light slants
through the bars of a cell grown familiar, an antici-
pated letter or visit from a friend or lover, a rough
blanket that has acquired the person's own scent from
constant use. The removal of such an item can be more
devastating than was the loss of the freedom of the
whole world outside. The man who looked with stony
eyes at the photographs of his father's funeral that his
stubbornness has kept him from attending, will weep
at the death of a moth that had briefly shared the lone-
liness of solitary with him.

Sibiza spent close to a year manufacturing chess
pieces out of the tinfoil wrappers from cigarette pack-
ages and chocolate bars. We discovered the painstakingly crafted figurines when he was still working on

the pawns, and we knew we had him. It was touching
the way he would carefully secrete his toys in a hol-
lowed-out wedge in his mattress (damaging state property, a serious offense!). We even have photographs of
the great man lost in contemplation of some pattern of
pawns and kings on the floor of his cell. Did we interrupt him in the pursuit of his hobby? Of course not.
To be exact, we allowed him to go on with it for one
hundred and twenty-two days.

At the end of this period, I had Sibiza taken without
warning from the exercise yard to a different cell—a
larger, brighter one with a new mattress. We let him
stew there for about a week and then brought him to
my office, where, sitting on my desk, was an attrac-
tively carved chessboard from one of the city's finest
crafts shops. On this board reposed his assiduous hand-
iwork. I watched his face carefully, but he sat down
without demur. In that instant of what should have
been *my* triumph the thought occurred to me that Sibiza had planned this all along, that he had never
doubted we were watching his every move. Or was this
just the impression he was trying to give me?

"Pawn to king four, Lieutenant," he said mockingly, advancing a hand to move the piece.

"I don't have time for idle games," I replied, exas-
perated. I was not about to satisfy him with a game of
chess.

He seemed, for once, disappointed. "You really
should play," he said wistfully. "When all the pieces
are moving in the right order and the plan laid out in
your head is unfolding before you, it is like a sym-
phony."

"Sibiza," I said. "If you renounce the Azanian Congress, you can go home and play all the games of chess
you want."

"Do you listen to symphonies, Lieutenant? Or do

you favor those quaint tribal melodies of yours?'' He grinned sardonically and began to whistle ''Suikerbossie.'' I'm ashamed to say that I cut the interview short, afraid that I might give in to my own anger. I felt pushed to the point where what I wanted most was to smash that broad and noble face, to feel the skin grow loose and pulpy beneath the onslaught of fist and boot and brass paperweight. I should have persisted with my reasoned arguments and pointed out yet again the clear fact that for the right word he could be a free man. I should not have let him see that he could best me in our war of nerves.

All this took place in the early days, for as time moved on Sibiza became too dignified to play games with his jailers. He is the only man I know to have grown in self-confidence behind bars. Like Antaeus, the more we threw him to the ground, the stronger he got.

Of course, there were always those in the outside world deceived and traitorous enough to want to help him. Why should Sibiza have felt alone and helpless in prison when that woman was willing to stand up in Parliament and make demands on his behalf? ''Why is Sibiza being denied access to the exercise yard?'' she would say. ''Is the wise and enlightened government of this great and powerful Republic afraid that he will flap his arms and soar over the prison walls?''

Sibiza, thank God, did not die at our hands. When the time came he passed peacefully, almost as if he were at home. I know, because I have seen the video-tapes. His wife was making her monthly visit and Sibiza was strolling at his usual stately pace toward her when he stumbled, put a hand to his chest, smiled apologetically at the surveillance camera, and crashed to the ground like a felled oak.

''I tried to reach him to hear his last words,'' N!omsa

Sibiza told the press later. "But there was that terrible plastic barrier that always kept us apart."

What nonsense! The man was dead before he hit the ground. The prison doctor was at his side the instant after the guard saw him fall but there was nothing to be done: as the *Golden Star* reported in five column headlines, the great heart had burst. No one can be blamed. Mortality happeneth to us all.

Of course, no opportunity for high drama is going to be passed up by his widow. You may recall the photographs of "a brutal police raid" on her house that made international news some years ago. I spoke to Van Rooyden, the policeman who appears to be striking the poor defenseless woman in that now-famous photograph. "I was standing there having a perfectly nice chat with her," he told me. "Then the newspapermen arrived and she leaped at me like she was going to scratch out my eyes!" The policeman's arm is raised to ward off a blow, not to strike one. This is just one more example of why we keep the press out of our trouble spots. If they will not act responsibly, then they will have to be curbed.

At the time of Sibiza's death, Mrs. Sibiza's histrionics were manifested by her stating to the press (we were allowing her unusual latitude and she took full advantage of it): "The police have poisoned my husband."

To prove she was wrong and to show our good faith, C.o.P. Krieger promised to let her have her own doctors present at the autopsy and to turn the body over to her for burial. I tried to get him to change his mind, saying that no good would come of it, but to no avail.

Events moved quickly. The doctors agreed that Sibiza had died of "myocardial infarction"; the funeral was scheduled; and crowds began to pour into the township despite our blockades. I witnessed the interment from the safety of a police helicopter high above the sea of angry mourners who were pressing forward for a final look at their leader. N!omsa threw herself on top of the coffin as it was being lowered into the ground and had to be pulled out of the grave by the ubiquitous beret-wearing "Sibiza Youths" who were keeping order in the crowd.

Watching through the binoculars as his family and close friends threw handfuls of dirt on the coffin, I felt a momentary twinge of sadness. I had known Sibiza for a long time and his passing was a painful reminder of my own eventual deterioration and dissolution as well. But I was relieved, too: a burden was gone, a dangerously insidious voice and presence was at last stilled, or so I thought. I felt the way a hunter does at the demise of some magnificent and terrible lion that has been terrorizing the countryside. As long as he was alive, no one was safe. Once he was dead, we could begin to feel sentimental about the passing of a challenging opponent.

I should have known that things are never so simple. There was continuing restlessness and anger among the population and we were forced to tighten up the roadblocks, to make arrests, to show that we will not be intimidated into relinquishing law and order. But a new and disturbing event has recently taken place: Sibiza's widow has disappeared from view, gone underground, somehow evading our ongoing surveillance of her and her cronies. Pamphlets have appeared in the townships declaring: "Sibiza Lives!" "Sibiza's Ideas Will Not Be Stopped!"

Rumor has it that, along with N!omsa, Sibiza's brain has gone underground as well. An informer at the Azanian Congress says they are planning to wire the brain to a computer and let the dead man's mind lead their long-awaited revolution. We quickly got hold of one of the doctors the widow had helping conduct the autopsy to check this nonsense out. Yes, he said, they had removed Sibiza's brain and given it to his spouse because she said she wanted something to remember him by. "There's nothing wrong with that. Surely you don't believe those crazy rumors? Why, it's impossible to hook up a living brain to a computer, let alone one preserved in formaldehyde."

We don't believe the rumors, but that is not the point. The African is a superstitious sort, and, as far as he is concerned, Sibiza's brain really does speak through the dead man's wife. There is renewed conviction on the faces of the township dwellers and the Ndooli story is repeated with each troublemaker that we bring in. For them, their leader truly is free and about to lead them to victory.

Someone has perpetrated a monstrous travesty to give the black man false hope. But we will not be made fools of, don't you worry. They may believe themselves invulnerable and think they can ignore our guns, but our guns will not ignore them. We will destroy the instigators of this new rebellion. We will find the brain of this dead man and we will lock it up again, far away where it can never do any more harm. We have no choice.

STORIES FROM A SOUTH AFRICAN BOYHOOD

FLATS, CATS, AND NEIGHBORS

There are four classes of inhabitant in the block of flats
where Mark Spiegelman lives with his parents, Charles
and Lena, and his brother, Joel. The social hierarchy is
not quite parallel with the physical layout of the building, for the penthouse is where the ''girls'' live—the
maids, nannies, and cooks who work six days a week
for the white families occupying the spacious apart-
ments below them. The servants' quarters on the roof
are unknown and forbidding territory for Mark; he
knows he is not supposed to go there, which makes the
place all the more intriguing. One day he overhears the
upstairs neighbor, Mrs. Mainzer, telling his mother
that there are ''bucks'' on the roof. Mrs. Mainzer emigrated from Germany the same year as his mother, but
she has a much stronger accent—perhaps because she
married a fellow German Jew and not a Scottish one—

and Mark often has trouble understanding what she says. However, he distinctly hears her use the word "bucks," and the temptation proves too much for him. Early the following morning, he climbs all the way to the top of the narrow iron staircase that leads to the building's summit, where he stops, impressed with his own adventurousness. A flash of white in a distant corner catches his eye; could this be one of the bucks? It moves again and he realizes that it is only a sheet on a clothesline flapping in the wind. Then he hears the voices of women talking in one of the African languages and he scurries quietly down the staircase, thinking: "I *almost* saw a buck."

Six months later, when his interest in birdwatching has many times led him to crawl through the wide drainpipes on the edge of the roof to watch the doves perform their mating dances and to scan the neighborhood for wheeling falcons, he thinks with embarrassment of his earlier excitement and he is glad that he told no one of his daring. Of course no antelope gallop across the cramped roofless corridors of the servants' quarters, though there are bed*bugs* and he has seen the "itchy bites" on their maid Doreen's arms that she plaintively bares to his mother's view.

Now he occasionally visits Doreen, bringing with him comics and the *Tarzan* books that his older sister gives him and which Doreen also loves to read. He enjoys his celebrity on the rooftop—the other maids often stopping by to ask after his parents or touch his blond hair ("Au, is soft, man"), not quite believing that it's real. The visits come to an abrupt end, though, when the caretaker complains to Mark's mother that "it's unhealthy for a child to be hanging around with natives."

On the next level down are the white families who preside over the three stories below the roof, the bulk of space in the complex. Mark's family lives on the first story, one flight over the parking garage, their front and back door just a few yards from the back stairs. It is a spacious, bright apartment with French windows opening onto the back corridor, and a veranda with a view of the front garden and the street. The doings of the great world can be viewed from this veranda : cars rushing by, pedestrians walking, the oak trees dropping their acorns onto the pavement, a roadgang pulling down one of the trees that is suffering from a blight—*Tsho tsholoza,* the foreman calls in a deep bass ; *Es' indaba,* the men sing back, grunting as their muscular bodies strain at the rope.

Next are the staff—the flat boys, the garden boys, the watchmen—who come in from the townships to start work before the white families wake up. The staff keeps changing, so their faces are often unfamiliar. They have a strange, wild smell that comes from traveling into the city on crowded buses. Mostly they work outside, away from the Spiegelmans' flat : washing the cars, sweeping the corridor, weeding the garden. Once a week, the flat boy rushes into the flat at seven and whisks away the Persian carpet in the dining room to hang it from the back stairs and beat it free of dust with a rattan carpet beater. (One day, Charles was standing on the carpet finishing an early morning cup of coffee when the flat boy rushed in and, as usual, yanked away the rug, almost toppling him in the process.) This job done, the man sweeps and then, on his hands and knees, polishes the wooden floor until it gleams and smells richly of linseed oil. Twice a week, the wash girl invades the flat. Since the Spiegelmans have a washer and dryer in the walk-in cupboard (long known to Mark as "the walking cupboard"), her main task is to iron the sheets, shirts, and trousers. Her ironing is not the reasonable and sedate activity Lena Spiegelman sometimes engages in when Charles needs a smart shirt for an early-morning meeting. Rather, it is a musical consortium of powerful rhythmic thumpings and muttered phrases. "One-and-one is master's soup, *thud!* Inkona kon 'yazi, sibe 'mfuti, *thump!* Peas-and-carrots is master's soup, *thud!* Umlungu wena hamba lo toilet, *bang!*"

Mark does not know most of the Africans who do outside work—the gardeners, the fellow who cleans the cars for an extra sixpence a week, the one who cleans the swimming pool. The exception is Suleiman the watchman, with whom he has a running feud. Mark would have just set himself up in a game of tennis against the garage wall (South Africa is forehand, England back), with S.A. winning five games to one in the first set, and there would be Suleiman rushing toward him. "Hey, you break-it the car, you break-it the window. *Hamba, wena. Suka!*" Mark would flee up the iron staircase to the first floor, from whose safety he would taunt Suleiman by calling him "The Magnificent." Mark does not know why his father has given the watchman this title, but he likes the sound of it and it never fails to make Suleiman furious.

One day, Suleiman succeeds in sneaking up on Mark while he is watching a weaver bird spin its nest in the tall willow on the other side of the wooden fence that forms the boundary between garden and garage. Suleiman seizes Mark tightly by the wrist, then seats himself on the edge of the open rain gutter.

"Why you always making-it troubles for me?" he asks.

"Let me go!" Mark yells, trying to twist out of the African's grip. This isn't in the rules of the game. "You're hurting me." Tears start in his eyes, but he doesn't want to let the watchman make him cry.

"All the time, the big missis, she say: 'Suleiman, you

let those children play, scratch-it the cars, make for big mess.' Yes, big troubles you make for me. Why you do it, this thing?''

"Suleiman," Mark responds, trying to achieve the tone of eminent reasonableness his mother acquires when explaining the finer points of starching to a new wash girl, "when have I ever broken anything in the garage? And I never leave rubbish lying around...." He wrenches his arm—almost free! "Let me go ... or I'll tell my father on you."

Suleiman shakes his head as if to say *he* is not taken in by empty threats. But Mark can see the realization slowly dawn on him: What if some white master or missis does come by and see him holding this child captive? Could he explain that he is just trying to teach the youngster a lesson?

Released, Mark walks off, rubbing his chafed wrist. "I don't like you, Suleiman," he says. "You're mean. I'm going to tell my father you were mean to me."

That night, though, he has practically forgotten the incident ... until his mother asks him how he came about the circular bruise on his left wrist.

"I don't remember," he says, hiding his hand under the edge of the table.

The fourth class of inhabitant is perhaps the freest, as well as the most despised. The feral cats that live in the rhododendron thicket behind the tennis courts neither commute, work, nor pay rent but remain residents despite Suleiman's best efforts to eradicate them. The cats use the intricate network of spill-over drains that traverse the sloping length of the apartment complex as their private road system. They are rarely seen during the day; though, every now and then, one might be lucky enough to see a cat dart to the storm drain from its resting place in the warm hub of a car's back wheel. But the most reliable indication of the continued exis-

tence of the cats' thriving colony are the banshee sere-
nades on warm nights and the occasional clumps of
downy feathers under a tree—the way the feathers ra-
diate outward in a semicircle making it look as if the
bird had spontaneously exploded. For Mark, the final
treat of an evening out at a restaurant or a school
performance is the slight glimpse—captured in the
mystical light of the car's headlamps as it climbs the
sloping driveway—of shadowy figures slipping in and
out of the doorless rubbish room. Although they keep
down the mouse population, the cats' messy raids on
the rubbish bins are undoubtedly the source of Suleiman's hostility toward them. Again it might be that,
like children, they upset his sense of order.

While Mark knew about the cats for a long time, it
was some years before he traced their presence to the
rhododendron bushes. This discovery comes to him
with that surprise of knowing that the puzzle's answer
has been right in front of you all along, had you simply
paused to ask the question sooner. After school, he now
deliberately walks the long way past the tennis courts,
hoping to see a tail disappear into the bushes or an
incautious kitten placidly watch his approach until
called to safety by its mother's frightened mew.

There is an underfed ginger tabby that, without
reflection, he names Ginger. This cat seems to be an
outcast—perhaps the last survivor from a litter
discovered by Suleiman—and the first time Mark sees
him is when Ginger, who is barely out of the kitten
stage, is forlornly licking at several fresh scratches
from a territorial quarrel. Mark skirts the outer perim-
eter of the path farthest from the thicket so as not to
disturb the cat. He hurries upstairs, returning with a
saucer of milk which he places near the spot where he
has just seen the cat. Then he retires some distance
away and sits down patiently to watch. After a few

minutes, Ginger emerges from the shrubbery and lies down in a patch of sunlight near the saucer, his wary eyes on Mark. He moves closer to the milk after a time, then dashes into the bushes, then reapproaches the saucer, closer this time. Eventually, thirst wins out over caution and he drinks from the saucer, every now and then raising his head in a silent, pitiful snarl.

Every day that week Mark puts out some milk, and every day he sits a little closer to watch the still uneasy cat perform its reconnoitering. Within two weeks, Mark is able to sit within touching distance while the animal feeds. He makes the mistake of reaching out to pet Ginger one day. Startled, the cat hisses fiercely and streaks off into the undergrowth. Mark is worried that he has destroyed its trust, but after he moves about ten feet away it returns to finish its dinner.

The old lady who lives in number 5, the closest flat to the rhododendron thicket, interrupts Mark twice the following week to yell at him: "Go away. What are you hanging about here for?" But, by the weekend, the delighted Mark is able to squat next to the saucer while Ginger, who has filled out and gives every sign of becoming a *big* cat, purrs contentedly and occasionally brushes against his legs.

Each day, Ginger grows more trusting, more delightful. On the way home from school, Mark can now stop and play with his friend even before he gets the animal's food. When he walks away, Ginger follows him, sometimes almost as far as the back stairs. Then, one afternoon, when Mark has stayed later than usual at school to take part in a pick-up soccer game, there is no cat to greet him at the bushes' edge. He notices a cracked bone china saucer in the place he usually leaves food for Ginger; the milk in it has started to congeal into yellow lumps in the sunlight. He returns with his own saucer of milk and puts it down, then wanders around the thicket calling out Ginger's name. The kitchen window of number 5 flies open and the old lady calls out: "Stop encouraging those animals, you horrible child," then slams the window shut to emphasize her words. Mark pushes his saucer into the vegetation to conceal it a little—the other saucer has mysteriously disappeared—then goes home.

Early in the morning, before school, he rushes over to check the bushes. The milk in the saucer is gone, but there is still no response to his calls. All day during school he cannot get his mind off his pet. He envisions the walk home through the mottled shadows of the tree-lined street, a left turn a few yards past the bougainvillea and then down the path that divides Eden Terrace from Eden Gardens, at the bottom of which lie the tennis courts and the rhododendron thicket. He can see the ginger-colored cat step confidently out of the bushes and come toward him to wind itself around his shins and rub the top of its head against his shoes. When he does get home, none of this happens.

A few days later, Mark is on his way to the garden when his upstairs neighbor, Brian, asks him to help look for Capone, the small white poodle Mark sometimes takes for walks. "I was playing tennis and he was running along the fence barking at the ball like he usually does, then he disappeared."

Mark likes Brian, a dark-haired, athletic eighteen-year-old who studies zoology at the university, and he is happy to help him search for the dog. "Capo-o-o-one," Brian cries, cupping his hand around his mouth. "Here, boy. Walkies!"

There is no sign of the dog. They walk around the tennis courts and then Mark decides to see how far he can go into the rhododendron thicket where it touches against the wire of the tennis courts. He has to balance on the brick edge of the rain gutter and pull himself along the crisscrossing wires while simultaneously moving aside straying branches. His progress is slow, and there is an unpleasant smell the farther he penetrates into the thicket. When he is several yards in, he sees the dog Capone coming toward him. But this is a different animal from the one he knows—Capone staggers as if intoxicated, retching all the way. A little farther back from the dog, Mark can make out a vague shape lying in the gutter; it is the size of a small animal. Mark backs up slowly, coaxing the dog to follow him, until they reemerge into daylight. Brian grabs his dog as soon as he sees it and starts running with it to his car, yelling that they've got to get Capone to the vet.

The vet at the animal hospital comes to see them in the waiting room. "Your dog's been pretty badly poisoned with arsenic trioxide, but it looks like we'll save him. What I want to know is how this happened. What was he eating?"

"My cat," Mark says. "He was eating my cat."

Mark tells Brian about the old lady and the strange cracked saucer with its blue oriental patterning. When they return to the Eden buildings, they go straight to number 5. Brian raps hard on her door with his bare knuckles, and as soon as the old woman opens he begins to shout at her: "Why did you poison this kid's cat? Now my dog's sick and I had to pay the vet forty rands."

"My bird ..." the old woman stammers. "Those cats killed my bird when I put his cage outside for air."

"You're crazy, lady. You're completely sick," Brian continues. "You can't go sticking poison all over the place. What if some child decided to drink that milk? What then?"

"I'm sorry," the white-haired woman murmurs, tears appearing in her eyes. "I wasn't thinking." She tries to pull her door closed, but Brian's foot is wedged firmly in the way.

"You're telling me you weren't thinking," Brian says, ignoring Mark who is now tugging at his shirt. "I ought to tell the police about you. You're a public menace!"

With a final "Ag, you disgust me," Brian moves his foot from the door and turns to go. The two of them walk away, but then Brian turns around again and shakes his fist at the old lady, who is watching them from behind the safety of her half-open kitchen window.

"You owe me forty rands," he roars.

THE CARETAKER

Mrs. Vogel, the caretaker of the Eden buildings, is a terrifying figure: an overweight, pasty-faced woman with curly white hair, she loves flowers and hates children. The garden is a profusion of blossoms: the frilly polls of hydrangeas nod above the well-tended flower beds; bougainvillea climb the wooden fences; and *Strelitzia africanus* wave their birdlike heads in the breeze. The grassy area where the neighborhood children play soccer is mowed twice a week and in the mornings a platoon of young African men move across the lawn on hands and knees, carefully removing each offending weed before it can flower.

One day, Old Voggie (as Doreen calls her) decides to protect her flower beds by having the servants place halved bricks edge-up along their borders. A few weeks later, Mark uses a sliding tackle to trap the soccer ball that his neighbor and friend, Lenny Mainzer, is dribbling toward the makeshift goals. Lenny is taken unawares and he trips, falling hard on the upturned bricks. The two boys gaze for a moment with detached curiosity at the deep, wedge-shaped gash in Lenny's upper leg. The flesh has been neatly parted as if by the blow of an ax and for a moment they can see the sinewy quadriceps muscle like a cheap cut of steak, the mat yellow layers of fat, and the white gleam of the fascia. Then an onrush of blood floods the wound and Lenny's piercing scream brings Mrs. Spiegelman running from the second-floor apartment. She scoops Lenny up in her arms and races with him to the car. Mark follows behind, amazed at his mother's strength; he has never seen her move so fast. Following her instructions, he sits in the back of the little Renault trying to hold his friend's flesh clamped tightly shut while his hands grow slippery with blood.

"I'm going to die. I'm going to die," Lenny wails, his thrashing-about causing blood to spray in all directions.

"Nonsense, you'll be just fine," Lena Spiegelman responds firmly, weaving between cars with the skill of a racing driver. "Just keep still. And, Mark, make sure you don't let that wound open up again."

"If you move, I'll sock you one," Mark says, fully prepared to knock his friend out as he has heard one should do with a drowning victim who starts to panic. Lenny stares in astonishment, tears coursing down his face, but he remains still all the way to Children's Hospital where a young doctor stitches him up, wraps a bandage around his leg and gives him a lime-green lollipop for being such a brave boy. Although the bricks still remain around the flower beds after Lenny's father has "a word with that monstrous woman," Voggie no longer shouts at the boys in her hoarse, Dutch-accented voice when she sees them playing on the grass. Instead, in uncharacteristically quiet tones, she asks them please to be careful.

DONALD

Words are what bring Mark and Donald Keller together. Before this happens, Donald is merely an irritating presence in the classroom, a know-it-all who is the only boy in Standard III to still play jacks with the girls. Donald's father gets more frequent mention in the Spiegelman household; for Nigel Keller, who is a pillar of the local synagogue, is also the public prosecutor conducting a high-profile treason trial against the politically active parents of two of Mark's school friends. He is usually not referred to by name but simply as "that bloody-minded hypocrite." So Mark is surprised when one of the teachers calls out young Donald for misbehaving by saying to the class: "He has such a brilliant father, and all he can do is play the fool."

Donald is by no means a deliberate michief-maker; rather, he is easily excitable and will do almost anything for attention. When Beatlemania sweeps through South Africa—each month bringing a new hit single on Springbok Radio and further vilification in the Afrikaner press—Donald appears at break with a portable gramophone, a plastic guitar, and his mop of unruly black hair combed forward over his forehead. "I wanna hold your ha-a-and," he mimes to the record, strumming frenziedly, while a small crowd of giggling Standard IV and V girls clap along in time.

One day, their regular teacher is sick, and the substitute, Mrs. Worth, tries to keep the class quiet by setting a particularly difficult spelling test. "Anyone who gets one hundred percent can go home early," she tells the class. To her unfeigned disbelief, there are two who get all the answers right: Mark and Donald.

"Are you going to walk home?" Donald asks Mark

when they were standing alone with their unexpected freedom outside the classroom.

"I dunno. I should wait for my brother." Mark kicks idly at the red brick wall next to the school gate. He watches a viceroy butterfly settle on a Namaqualand daisy and unfurl its long proboscis. It is spring, a beautiful day, the jacaranda trees in full blossom. "Nah, let's go. My mom can come and pick up Joel anyway." He knows that Donald's house is just a few blocks from his own turnoff onto Eden Road.

"I bet you think you know a lot of words?" Donald says as they walk along, taking idle pleasure in the free gift of an extra hour of unscheduled time.

"I *do* know a lot of words," Mark insists.

"*Ostentatious?*" Donald says, his voice a challenge.

"Snobby, sort of . . . I think."

Donald smiles in a superior way. "*Constitution,*" he says. "If someone says you have a good constitution?"

"It means you're healthy." That was an easy one, his mother often says it's lucky she has a good constitution. Ostentatious, he's a lot less sure of. Now it's his turn. "*Nictitating? Vestigial?*"

Donald shakes his head. Mark knows these words aren't really fair; he'd found them in his snake book the night before. He is a voracious reader of animal books and he keeps a list of unusual zoological terms and animal names.

"You couldn't be expected to know that," he now tells Donald. "I only just looked them up myself."

They talk about their favorite books the rest of the way—both of them like *Tarzan* and *The Hardy Boys* —and when they reach the turnoff, Donald suddenly grasps and shakes Mark's hand in an oddly adult gesture and says: "See you in school tomorrow?"

Before Mark has a chance to reply, Donald notices that the traffic light is in his favor and runs across the

street. He keeps walking, but turns to wave goodbye
several times.

They don't really become good friends during school
—Donald still doesn't join the wild running games of
Robbers versus Thieves led by the boys from the Jew-
ish orphanage—but a barrier has been washed away
and they occasionally walk home together. One evening, Mark gets an unexpected phone call from Donald: "My mother says I can have a friend stay over
tomorrow night. Can you come?"
Late the following afternoon, Mark is dropped off at
the Kellers' home, an imposing brick house with a semi-
circular driveway surrounded by dense bushes. In his
SAA airline bag he carries pajamas, a toothbrush, a
shirt for the next day, and three books: one that he has
almost finished and two more because he is not sure
which to begin next. It is the first time he has ever slept
at a friend's house and he wonders what sort of things
one does; it seems like an adventure, stepping into
other people's lives this way.
The visit begins ordinarily enough; Donald gives
Mark a tour of the capacious house and the large
grounds in the back, then the two settle in Donald's
room to read comics, of which he has a sizable collection. They are discussing their favorite issues of *Bat-
man* when Donald suddenly announces: "I must have
a snooze." Mark is about to tell Donald "You sound
just like my dad," but the other boy has already lain
down on the white cotton coverlet of his bed, his black
school shoes still on his feet, and begun to snore. Now
and then, he mumbles something in his sleep. Mark
watches him for a few minutes hoping he'll wake up,
then returns to the comic he was reading before. About
twenty minutes later, Donald leaps up and walks
quickly and determinedly straight into the closed door.

"What happened?" he asks, looking dazedly around him.

"You fell asleep, then you walked into the door."

"How very odd." Donald responds. He lies down on the bed again, breathing slowly and deeply, then gets up again after a few minutes looking refreshed.

"You should put some ice on that." Mark gestures toward Donald's forehead, where an egg-shaped bump is beginning to appear.

"Oh, I'll be fine," his friend responds, sitting down beside him.

Donald's parents arrive a little after six and his mother comes into the bedroom to say hello. She is a small, mouse-haired woman with a timid smile. She tells Mark several times that it is very nice he could stay over for the night, then announces that they can take supper in the kitchen anytime they are ready. They pass Dr. Keller (who does not heal the sick but is a Doctor of Jurisprudence) on their way into the kitchen—a squat, gray-haired man with tired eyes who nods briefly in their direction. They are promptly served cottage pie and baby peas by a coloured maid in a spotless white uniform who keeps her eyes downcast and calls each of them "young master."

"Don't you eat with your parents?" Mark asks. He is only banished from the dining table when there are important guests and often not even then.

"Sometimes. Anyway, I can't watch my father eat," Donald says. He takes on the look of a heron hunting for fish as he imitates his father's rapid, precise, and finicky gestures, eyes glinting as they dart around the plate in search of fresh morsels. Mark suddenly recalls that, during lunch break, Donald would usually take his sandwich a little distance away from the others and eat it with his back turned.

• • •

Mark's favorite treat on his birthdays is to go to Maria's farm. Maria is a beautician who employed Lena when she first came to the country from Germany and who taught her how to do facials and manicures. Mark has overheard his parents say that Maria "runs with a rough crowd," which sounds interesting, although he is not sure what it means. This year his mother suggests that they have a birthday party at home, saying that she has not been in touch with Maria all year and that it's not nice to call someone only when you want something from them. She eventually gives in to his nagging, however, and on the Saturday following his birthday, two station wagons loaded with children set out for the farm, which lies an hour outside of Johannesburg. In the car driven by his mother are Mark, Lenny Mainzer, Michael Lasker, and Donald Keller. In the other car, driven by Lenny's mother, are Mark's little brother, Joel, Clive and Martin Goldberger, and Mark's best friend, David.

The farm is as beautiful as ever, in a way that only land left untended to can be beautiful. What was once a field of lucerne is now a scraggy patchwork of brush and wildflowers, scarred by the careless, looping trails of horses given their leads. Flycatchers and drongos dart after leaping insects and a seemingly drunk chicken runs a zigzag course directly in front of the car. Maria, however, seems unrelaxed and not particularly happy to see them. She gives Mark a distracted kiss on the side of his head and wanders back to where several youngish men in khakis are lounging around a rough wooden bench. One of them argues with her, then joins her to greet Mark's mother and Mrs. Mainzer.

"This is Rudi," Maria says proudly.

"Hullo," he says, his hands in his pockets. Rudi is all sharp edges, with hard gray eyes and short-cropped hair. He looks off into the distance with deliberate casualness, then turns on his heel and walks back to his companions.

"He's worried that the children will interfere with his shooting," Maria says indulgently, "but I promised they'd stay out of his way."

There are only two aging mules for the children to ride, two per animal. Since it is his birthday, Mark gets to go first, although he offers to wait while one of the others rides. He sits uncomfortably—the Basuto blanket covering the hard saddle makes his bare legs itch— and holds tightly onto the reins, even though an aged and barefooted African wearing the brim of a hat leads the way. Behind him, young Martie Goldberger says in a loud whisper: "Why'd *he* have to come along?"

"He's a nice guy, really. You just have to get to know him," Mark responds, glancing over at the other donkey to see whether Donald heard the remark intended for him. He tries to take pleasure in the sun on his face, the grasshoppers leaping to either side, the sight of a *springhaas* leaping away from its disturbed resting place, but his enjoyment seems effortful and, increasingly, he is getting saddle sore. It is a relief, then, to see the crude huts of the farm, its long dining bench sheltered by a woven grass roof, where the others are gnawing at stringy boiled chicken (the same one that performed its dance in front of the car?) and eating potato salad.

The sounds of men's laughter, the sharp crack of a .22 rifle, and distant splintering of beer bottles drift over the lunch table. Mark watches his mother and Maria engaged in earnest conversation: Lena looks especially cheerful and serene beside Maria with her flickering eyes, dyed blond hair, and tight-lipped smile.

"Hurry up, slow-coach," Michael Lasker says. "I want to go shooting with the *ous*."

The two of them walk past the toolshed, where several of the men are sprawling in the shade, and go around the back to where a fleshy young man is shooting badly at a row of beer bottles strung dangling by their necks from a tree limb. A tall and athletic man with a swatch of leopard skin around his hunter's cap is watching him, chuckling each time he misses.

"Let me have a shot," Mark says.

"Voetsek, you," the stout man replies, wiping his forehead with a dirty cravat. He has the sour smell that fat people who sweat easily sometimes get.

"Come on, Wim," the other man laughs. "You're never going to hit anything anyway."

Wim hands the rifle to Mark, who aims it carefully, trembling a little because the gun is heavier than he is used to. He squeezes the trigger, and is almost knocked over by the kick of the butt against his shoulder. The shot goes wild. "You've got to hold it tight against your shoulder and shoot low," Michael says, steadying the barrel for him so he can fire a second shot. This time one of the bottles bursts, seeming to explode on its own before the crash of the rifle can be heard. The fat man stalks off in disgust. Mark's arm throbs and he knows there will be a bruise later, but he is glad that he didn't give up with the first try.

As they are walking past the toolshed later, Rudi calls after them. "Hey, boys, you want to see something funny?" It takes a moment for their eyes to adjust to the shadows in the hut after the bright sunlight outside, but then they can see what the men are laughing about. They have caught a bat and nailed its spread-eagled wings to a broad plank of wood. Someone has stuck a cigarette into the animal's open mouth, and as it struggles, the lit end glows as if the bat is enjoying a good smoke.

"That's horrible," Mark cries. "Let it go at once!"

"You're a sissy," Rudi says, turning his cold eyes on Mark.

"And you're a pig...hurting a poor animal like that."

Rudi stares at Mark in fury, muscles tensed to hit him. Mark is shocked at himself; he's never been this impolite to an adult before. But the athletic man with the hunter's hat lays a restraining hand on Rudi's arm and remarks: "He's got you peeped, that's for sure. He's really got you peeped."

A slow smile appears on Rudi's face, making him almost likable. "Come on, get out of here. Bugger off, then," he says, his tone not unfriendly.

Mark does not tell his mother about the smoking bat on their ride home and she, too, is preoccupied. "The farm's not like I remember it," he suddenly blurts out, and Lena smiles, for they often have a way of expressing each other's thoughts. There is birthday cake waiting for them on their return, a surprise from Doreen, and there is a general brightening of the partygoers' spirits. Even the Goldbergers and Donald seem to get along without incident. The children then go and play soccer in the front garden while they wait for their mothers to pick them up. Helen Goldberger—who was recently told by Donald's father that she could leave the country if she wished, but her children could not— arrived at the same time as Mrs. Keller.

"Donnie, Donnie," Sophie Keller calls from inside the car, trying to ignore the other woman, who is gazing at her with mingled fury and pity. As she drives off, Donald leans out the passenger window and waves at the remaining partygoers like a politician at a motorcade.

Mark spends one more night sleeping over at the Kellers'. When Lena pulls up to the driveway to drop him off, a policeman armed with a submachine gun stops her. ''There've been some threats against the doctor,'' the policeman tells her, asking the reason for her visit. Mark can tell by the tilt of her head as she drives away that his mother is not pleased. Donald, on the other hand, is delighted with the police presence. After supper they go into the back garden and talk to the policemen, one of whom is holding a German shepherd on a leash. He hands Mark a matchbox and says: ''Here, bury this anywhere in the garden and Scout will find it.'' The boys borrow a torch from the policeman, take a shovel from the gardener's shed, and dig a hole in the soft earth below the mulberry tree. They stand for a moment in the dark, enjoying the scent of fermenting mulberries and the quiet rustling of sleepy birds in the branches.

''He'll never find it,'' Donald says flatly when they return to the back porch.

''*Yussus,* you wait and see,'' the policeman says. He whispers in the dog's ear and releases it. The police dog courses along the hedge, nose to the ground, before disappearing into the obscurity. A few minutes later it reappears with dirt on its forepaws and the matchbox in its mouth. The boys try it again, hiding the object in the limb of a tree, in the shed, under stones, but each time the olfactory genius of the German shepherd wins out.

Afterward, they play a new game imported from America that was given to Donald by his Israeli cousins. A little plastic man points with a cane to various questions on a board. After you have written down your answers, you place the man on a mirrorlike sheet of metal and he swivels around to magically point at the correct answer. By twisting the loose paper covering the board, they are able to make the man give the wrong answers, and they stay up late laughing at the ridiculous results. There are sounds at the front door, and the boys click off the light and dive into bed before Donald's parents can discover that they are still up. Mark occasionally wakes during the night to the sound of the measured tread of the young policeman and his dog patrolling the back garden.

The late edition of the next day's *Star* reports that an unexploded bomb was found at the edge of Nigel Keller's house that morning. Charles Spiegelman is infuriated. "No son of mine is going to get blown up in that bastard's house," he fumes.

Several months later, Mark is invited to a birthday party at Donald's house. The party is in the back garden and there are a lot of guests : the boys—their wetted-down hair slowly returning to its natural state of disorder—are wearing dapper long-sleeved shirts that still bear creases where they were folded; the girls are in soft pastel dresses. Picnic tables have been set up with cold drinks and triple-layer ice-cream cakes.

"Time for the lucky dip," Dr. Keller calls out in his soft, even voice. "Line up next to me here. First come, first served. Don't forget to shut your eyes."

Each child shuts his or her eyes and reaches into the sack that Donald's father holds open. Mark feels the various packets inside the bag : all are full and bulging with mysterious treats. "You've got to make your choice," Dr. Keller says. "Others are waiting."

Mrs. Keller wanders around the garden smiling shyly at each child, watching as they open their lucky packets, helping to cut the cakes that are losing their shape as the afternoon wears on. Dr. Keller oversees the games—fishing with magnets, the three-legged race —and after each one there is a prize. The egg-and-spoon race is about to begin when there is a dispute : Donald's fish, which held the highest number, fell off

the magnet and bounced against the rim of the ''fish
bowl'' only to drop back inside. Donald insists that he
deserves the prize because he did get the fish all the
way out of the bowl.

''Donald,'' his father says in his usual monotone.
''That will be enough.''

''But I caught it, I tell you! I caught it.''

''Come inside, boy.''

''But, Dad . . .''

It is too late; his father is already walking toward
the house. Donald follows resignedly. Just as they
reach the back door, Dr. Keller turns and says in his
quiet voice: ''Carry on, children.''

The participants in the race collect their tablespoons
and hard-boiled eggs and line up at the starting line
where Mrs. Keller is standing. Then, through the open
window of Donald's bedroom comes the swish of a belt
and a sharp crack. ''No, Dad, ouch. Stop it, please,
Dad.'' Donald's voice floats in the clear afternoon air,
punctuated by the swish and snap of the belt against
bare skin. His voice sounds bored, as does that of his
father telling him to be good.

''Come on, children. Keep on with the race,'' Mrs.
Keller begs but is ignored while they stand in fascination, avoiding looking at each other's faces. The sounds
coming from the house soon cease and Donald reappears, his father close on his heels.

''So who won?'' Donald asks, looking with calm interest at his uncertain friends caught frozen in a pose
on the green lawn.

THE WIDOW

Mark dreads the visits to Anna Litchfield's house, which is filled with hazards of all kinds. She owns three tan Great Danes, more horse than dog, whose lolling tongues and sharp canines are at eye level. "Don't show any fear and they won't bother you," she tells the children, who dare not even flinch when a gigantic, hot, wet tongue slaps against their faces. Hers is no green, shaded lawn but a cactus garden with every variety of sticking plant and every vegetable means of piercing flesh: a green succulent's waving swordlike fronds that end in a single needle-sharp thorn and leave an itchy, beaded string of blood on one's unprotected calf; the intricately meshed stiletto blades of the wait-a-bit tree; the blunt phalloi of a rare cactus from the Namib desert; a small, well-concealed cactus's tiny hairs that irritate to distraction and have to be carefully picked out of the skin with tweezers; and the barbed fishhooks of the jumping cholla.

Anna Litchfield, the owner of this forbidding estate, is a thin woman with a dry, raspy voice whose kindnesses always seem vaguely menacing. She blows cigarette smoke in the children's faces as they nibble at the sugary biscuits she offers them at teatime. Anna herself is not given to seeing the funny side of things, but she is dogged by a sardonic devil and her many misfortunes always have a memorable ironic twist. After her first husband, Heinrich Haas, was killed in a traffic accident, for example, the policeman who was to inform her of this disaster showed up at the door and asked: "Excuse me, are you the widow Haas?"

Shortly after Anna Litchfield—who reverted to using her maiden name after her husband's death—opens an outdoor Vienna-style Kaffeehaus in the Killarney Centre, she invites Lena and the children to join her there for coffee and cake. Lena's coffee is served in an elegant silver-and-glass decanter, but the "cake" consists of those same homemade shortbread biscuits with their granular dusting of sugar.

"I saved a life yesterday," the widow discloses without preamble. "I was visiting Clea Muller, who, you might remember, lives with her sister Beatrice in Hillbrow."

"I was in school with Bea," Mark's mother remarks. "She was always a bit odd. She spent a couple of years in Tara."

Tara was the insane asylum outside of Johannesburg. Some of Mark's teachers threaten unruly pupils that they will wind up there.

"Ja, she thought she was being persecuted. She claimed her husband was hypnotizing her."

"Poor man," Lena says. "He was always so nice. He couldn't understand she was ill."

At that moment Anna's attention is distracted by several small black children who are slipping in and out among the tables stealing the packets of sugar that are stacked in cups on each table.

"Hey, Hamba. You, *voetsek!*" she shouts, giving chase. She soon returns, wiping imaginary sweat from her brow. "They plague me, you've got no idea. The way things are now."

"So how did you save Beatrice's life?" Lena asks. On the trail of a good anecdote, Mark's mother is not one to give up easily.

"Well, when I got there, you know, Clea met me at the door. Hysterical, absolutely hysterical. Bea had locked herself in the bathroom with a paring knife and was threatening to cut her wrists. ..."

"So what did you do?"

"I told her that I had to use the bathroom and unless

she opened the door I would do it right there on the floor.''

Mark and his mother cannot repress their smiles at her ingenuity, but Anna does not see the joke. Of course no well-brought-up German girl, however desperate, could bear the thought of a guest fouling the hallway.

TRAVELING COMPANIONS

Like an attacking army, the Spiegelmans always set out before dawn when going on holiday. The hastily gulped hot chocolate spreading a warm glow inside them, Mark and Joel bundle on the woolen sweaters Lena knitted for them, fill their satchels with books and comics for the journey, and hurry outside. They stand beside the car, stamping their feet and blowing dragon's breath at each other in the chill Highveld air, while Charles arranges and rearranges the suitcases in the boot.

On this particular trip, there will be additional passengers along with the family. The widow Haas has taken an interest in the care and education of her African maid's two young sons, and she has asked Charles to drop off the children at their grandmother's in Zululand. Just as Charles, who wants to avoid the morning rush hour, is beginning to complain about the delay, the widow's old black Humber pulls up and deposits two subdued and bleary-eyed children. They are dressed in gray wool jerseys, threadbare discards that still bear the distinctive imprint of King Alfred's, the best-known rival to Mark and Joel's own school. The two Africans tremble slightly in the cold and hurry wordlessly into the car as soon as Charles opens the back door.

At first Skollie and Witbooi sit quietly between Joel and Mark, and all four children kneel on the backseat to watch in awe as the flat orange disc of the sun rises slowly over the city behind them and turns the lifeless mat-yellow mine dumps into hills of burnished gold. But as the day warms, so the two Africans become more rambunctious. Skollie surreptitiously pokes and pinches Mark, who is trying to read his new Classic

Comic of *Ivanhoe*. Witbooi drums his feet against the seatback in front of him until Charles, holding on to the steering wheel with his right hand and slapping blindly and indiscriminately in the backseat with his left, threatens to "turn around and go home." Trying to suppress his giggles, Witbooi explodes in a shower of snot, which he heedlessly wipes with his sleeve, while little Joel, who is finicky to the last, withdraws as much as he can into the corner. Skollie then tries to distract Joel by looming close and making google-eyes at him. Bored with this sport, he and his brother play a slapping game with their hands, murmur obscene-sounding phrases in Zulu, shake with silent laughter.

Midmorning, they stop at a roadside tearoom. Charles parks the car under a tall elm at the edge of the dusty culvert and leaves Lena there with the children while he goes inside the faded brick building.

"I want to go inside," Joel complains. "It's cold out here."

"We're having a picnic," Lena replies. "It'll be fun."

"I don't want a picnic. Why can't we go inside?" he whines, willful now that they are no longer trapped inside the moving car, and in that moment Mark understands that it is because of *them* that his father has deviated from the usual holiday routine. Of course, in this dorp the servant's children would have to go around to the back while the family sat comfortably inside.

"We never do what I want, we never do what I want," Joel sings rhythmically, stomping round and round the tree while Lena begs him to stop because he's giving her a headache. Both cheer up when Charles comes back with a thermosful of weak, hot tea sweetened with condensed milk. It is this rather insipid concoction that seems always to herald the true beginning of every holiday, the moment when you realize that you have left behind the sophistication of the city and have to adjust to country—or, more exactly, Afrikaner—ways. Cottage pie, tea or coffee that is syrup sweet with a gooey swirl of condensed milk at the bottom of the cup, not-quite-cold bottles of Pepsi encased in a sticky layer of grime . . . this is the exotic fare of the no-man's-land beyond Johannesburg.

After tea and Lena's cream-cheese-and-chutney sandwiches, Mark's parents take the car to fill the petrol tank and check the radiator, leaving the children to amuse themselves at their picnic spot. For a while they play a game of pitch-penny with some small pebbles they gather near the tree. Skollie is by far the most accurate, and he has soon assembled a small pile of the stones at his feet. Nonchalantly, he picks one up and cricket-bowls it toward the parking lot, where it bounces off the roof of a car with a loud *ping!*

"Don't do that," Mark says, shocked. Smiling mischievously, Witbooi picks up a sharp-edged piece of gravel and tosses it in the direction of the tearoom. *Chock!* Skollie throws another pebble accurately at the corrugated tin roof of the white-brick building.

"The police will come and arrest you," little Joel declares. The two African children instantly lose their buoyancy. They glance nervously at each other, and Mark notices all of a sudden how thin and ill fed they look.

"If the police come, you must tell them *you* did it," Witbooi insists.

"But that's not telling the truth," Joel replies with indignation.

"You *must*," Skollie says hoarsely. "You have to . . . for us."

Just then Charles returns with the car and the conflict is resolved as quickly as it has begun, though Witbooi and Skollie continue to look around for some time afterward to make sure no police cars are following.

As the day warms, the children grow more and more sleepy. Mark leans his head against the side of the door and shuts his eyes. The car's vibration make his teeth rattle, but it is not unpleasant, and after a while he falls asleep. Dazed and too warm, he dimly feels Witbooi slump against him, the African child's hot face pressed against his upper arm. Mark's bare leg starts to feel sticky and wet; Witbooi is asleep with his mouth wide open, a thin stream of saliva trickling out of it. Mark tries gently to extricate himself, but the other boy mutters in protest and snuggles closer. Conscious of his martyrdom and vaguely ashamed of the desire to hysterically mop at the damp patch on his leg, Mark closes his eyes again.

The outside air grows warmer and more humid, and after some time they find themselves driving through fields of waving sugar cane. Flying insects throng in the air and are slaughtered by the onrushing automobile, each tiny body crying *a life! a life!* as it leaves its yellowish smear on the windscreen. The road winds around as it climbs into the hills, the motion making the children nauseous despite the drier, crisp air. At last they drive into a small compound of mud-and-wattle huts where the car stops and is quickly surrounded by shrill and laughing children. Skollie and Witbooi scramble out and are quickly lost in the crowd. As Charles turns the car around, several of the children gape and point at Mark and Joel, but Mark is no longer able to distinguish which of them had spent the morning in the car with them. Perhaps Skollie and Witbooi are in that group that are already moving toward the hut, not bothering to look back, excited only to be home once more.

THE RAID

The knock at the door comes at five-thirty sharp. Peremptory, insistent, it startles the household into wakefulness. Mark and Joel stumble out of their bedroom in their pajama bottoms to peer with sleepy, astonished eyes at the khaki-clad policemen who fill up the kitchen with their bulk. The policemen, for their part, are disarmed by Lena's calm hospitality.

"You must be hungry, Sergeant. What can I offer you for breakfast?" she says, as if predawn visits by policemen are an everyday occurrence.

Mark goes into his parents' bedroom, where his father is frantically scurrying around grabbing handfuls of potentially damaging letters and papers that he has been meaning each day to destroy. He stuffs these into a briefcase which he presses onto his older son. "Take this to school with you," he says. "And don't let it out of your sight, not even for a minute."

Charles is the first to leave the flat. This is a busy week for him as one of the heads of the Institute for South African Legal Studies—a research institution critical of the government's increasing encroachment against what was once an independent judiciary—and he has to be at work, raid or no raid. He is glad to see that these are youngish policemen in the dining room: their forks gripped awkwardly in their big hands while they enjoy Lena's excellent curried scrambled eggs. It means that this is intimidation, not a serious move to put the Institute out of action. Still, he is worried. You never know what they might find, what they might consider incriminating.

When it is Mark's turn to leave, he feels himself grow flushed as he and Joel walk past the two policemen, his school satchel in one hand, the bulging briefcase in the other. They pay no attention to him, and his mind can now turn to the unpleasant task of explaining as little as possible to the inquisitive Mrs. Mainzer why she should drive them and her son Lenny to school although it is not her turn in the car pool.

Lena is left to watch the policemen make a mess of her clean house: dumping her clothes drawers out onto the bed to sift through her underwear for hidden contraband, pulling the books off the bookshelves, checking the bottoms of the lamps for hidden transmitters. She remembers with sudden horror that the next-to-bottom drawer contains some things she would not want the police to find—a letter from a close friend who was a member of the South African Communist Party, a brooch with a black hand clasping a white hand and the letters ANC engraved on it, Mandela's letter to Charles praising the Institute. She has noticed their method of pulling all the drawers in her wardrobe open and shutting each one as they finish going through it. When they near the offending drawer, she calls the terrified Doreen in and tells her to serve the policemen coffee in the dining room.

"I need to get dressed," she says firmly. "As you can see, I am still wearing my nightgown."

She hurriedly gets dressed, first pulling out the drawer she does not want them to see and exchanging it with one they have already examined. Then she serves the policemen biscuits, which Doreen has neglected to do, and asks them about their families.

All morning the phone rings, the very first caller being a journalist who says: "I hear Charles has been picked up. Do you know what the charge is?"

Lena wonders if Charles had been detained when he arrived at work, whether the journalist knows something, is second-guessing, or simply trying to prod her for information. She calls the Institute, but all the lines are busy, and none of the other people who call have any more definite knowledge of Charles's fate. Lena hears that there have been raids all over town; the government is casting a wide net this time and suddenly no one is safe, no matter how prominent or reputable they are.

"No," she says to one caller after another. "I don't know if they've closed down the Institute." "No, I don't know what the charges are." "Thank you, Mr. Friedman. I'm delighted you want to represent us, but why don't we see what's going on first." Lena would love to leave the phone off the hook, but she does not dare in case her husband calls.

All the while, the police are carefully examining every item in the rooms where the Spiegelmans have spent the past ten years of their married life. They ask her about each entry in her checkbook. "Who is this Marvin Goldstein that you pay one hundred and ten rand to every month? Does he belong to an illegal organization?"

"It's the rent," she responds, seeing the disbelief on the policeman's face that anyone would pay so much. He looks around the flat with more respect, but continues his diligent inquiries. "I see. What did you buy at Belfast's for thirty rands?"

At work, Charles too is kept busy by policemen who are swarming all over the building. They field every incoming phone call and politely tell him he may not make any calls out. "It's my work," he tells them. "What do you think I do all day?" But to no avail. Each wastepaper basket is emptied and carefully combed through, each file examined. When Charles sees them taking Jonathan Peters, an innocuous young clerk from the filing department, out of the building in handcuffs, he calls in the senior officer.

"What is going on here? How do you expect us to

get anything done if you arrest every clerk we have?"
he demands angrily. "I can assure you that Jonathan
Peters hasn't done anything, and, anyway, you should
arrest me if you have a problem with the Institute...
not the underlings."

"And I can assure you, Mr. Spiegelman, that our
charges against Mr. Peters are very serious indeed."

Charles finds out from the following day's newspapers that a small band of amateur anarchists led by
Peters have been making homemade bombs in the back
shed of the clerk's house. At Peters's trial, months
later, a munitions expert testifies that there "isn't a
hope in hell that these bombs would do more than make
a loud bang. They would have been better off buying
thunder crackers on Guy Fawkes Day." Peters is sen-
tenced to ten years at the close of the trial; the munitions expert is reprimanded for levity.

Mark's day is uneventful. No one asks him about the
fat briefcase he lugs around with him, and even Lenny
is uncommonly quiet about what he suspects is going
on at the Spiegelmans' flat. When Mark gets home in
the early afternoon, Lena is making the policemen sign
receipts for every item they are confiscating: the
banned books, the typewriters, the Hebrew prayer
books they are convinced are communistic documents.
The policemen thank her when they leave and wish her
a pleasant afternoon.

THE WITNESS

The sun is still warm on my face, but I can feel the first breezes of the late afternoon, promising a chill evening. The Mahotella Queens are singing on the radio in a nearby yard, and I can hear a woman softly crooning along with their song as she washes her clothes. Water splashes plaintively against the sides of the galvanized metal bucket. I can hear the thump of cloth being beaten clean and smell the soapy trickle of suds dribbling into our yard. An insect tickles at the corner of my mouth. I brush it away, but soon it reappears, buzzing loudly, circling to land again. I wait until I can just feel the soft breath of its wings on my face; then I swiftly grasp it in midair. The fly struggles against the enclosing dark, its feathery legs grasping and pulling at the cracked calluses of my palm. I wait until it is calm, accepting its prison now that nothing worse seems to be going to happen to it, then I slowly unfurl my fingers. The creature hesitates, perhaps checking itself for damage, and then the tiny weight lifts from my flesh and is gone.

I rise and go inside the house. The latch of the door is the height of my waist and is encased by a dry shell of children's snot. The house smells of children, dust, *mielie pap*. I gather up my greatcoat and stocking cap, go into the kitchen, and spoon some cold porridge into my tin lunch bucket from the large pot of pap that stands in the coolest corner of the kitchen. Now I am ready to make my way to the prison.

As I am leaving, I pass Ma Thlaka at the front gate where she is talking to a woman whose voice I do not know.

"See you tomorrow," I say.

"Ja, have a good evening," she responds.

The strange woman must think I cannot hear as well, for she does not wait for me to be gone before she murmurs, "Shame." As my feet tread firmly along the familiar route, the smell of cooking fires wafting above the township's usual odor of burnt rubber and human waste makes me hungry. It leads me to wonder if Meerkat will be cooking something on his brazier in the vacant lot tonight. Last week, the flying ants appeared after it rained—not so numerous now as when we used to be surrounded by veld, but enough to supply us with a good feast. I could taste childhood with each sweet crunch of the tiny brittle bodies, remembering what it was like to see them rise magically from the damp ground and whir into the air, which was already filled with darting predatory birds. That was a long time ago, before the illness that first dimmed and then shut off the bright rays of the sun, before I learned to see without having sight.

Children are whispering and giggling somewhere near me. I sense a small figure dancing in front of me

... probably making foolish faces and gestures, too. Something touches me on the shoulder. Ag, they are throwing rubbish again. *"Pas op,"* I warn, raising my stick. The giggling grows louder but the footsteps begin to recede. Once I got angry and lashed out with my stick fast enough to slash the bare legs of a little girl who squealed and began to cry with little wailing intakes of breath. My ear stung suddenly and grew hot. Another stone grazed my cheek, a third dug into my shoulder blade and then an adult voice shouted: "Simon, mBongi, Vusi, *laat die arme dingus rus,* you *bliksems."* Leave the poor thing alone ... and they did, though it is not often that they listen these days.

There is a rumbling behind me and I move swiftly to the side of the road, my foot sinking to the ankle in a wet ditch. The lorry roars past, accompanied by the cheerful shouts of the soldiers inside who are heading away from this jumble of menace and erupting stones. It is not wise to dream too much while the army is about; if you don't scurry for cover, they think you are up to something.

There are no sounds from Meerkat's lot. I stir his brazier with my stick but the ashes are almost cold. It has been some days since he was last here, though he said nothing about leaving. Who knows where he is? The nights have been cold, it is true, but Meerkat always knows where to find some wood for his fire, although that too gets harder and harder. Of course, he may have been picked up. How surprised he would be to find himself riding in my elevator. But they would not bring him to Hendrijkslied Prison for a pass violation.

I have known Meerkat for how long? Three years, I think, and he has always told me before if he was going away. I wonder what they could want from him? His hands are strange to touch, the left is like a flattened flipper and there are only two fingers on his right hand.

His sleeve caught in the big roller at the factory and the machine began to pull him in like a hungry crocodile until the white boss flicked the off switch. Meerkat likes to talk about the time just after the accident. "Those were *lekker* times," he would say, "when I had my *kompensayshun*. No boy's meat for me and brandy every night." What trouble could he get into with those hands?

I am near the train station, now. Hearing the cheerful voices of the first men to start coming home. It is Friday, payday, but it is still light and the working men are in sufficient numbers not to feel afraid of the *tsotsis*. The later ones will not be so lucky, or, at least, the lucky ones will be those who don't give up their lives with their pay packets. Even the tsotsis are hungrier these days. I have pretended not to notice the furtive fingers that quickly explored my empty pockets, ignored the spittle or cuff of the man who is only angry at himself for not realizing that I would not be likely to have money. On the platform, I stand near some women who are going into the city to clean up in those new high-rise office buildings. I like the smell of their starched and clean overalls, their loud chatter and humorous remarks about male anatomy. They take no shame about discussing me in my presence. "They have sensitive fingers," one says. "Cause they have to touch everything to know what it is."

"Yussus, my man doesn't know what fingers are. Just pull out the ol' dingus and dig away like he's trying to get gold out of a rock."

"Soon's he's done, mine wants his dinner," another says.

Their talk stirs me. One has a pleasant voice; cheerful fat quivers in her laughter. I would like to touch their faces, trace the outlines of their bodies, smell their arousal. But I know they would find my touch too

serious, too searching a thing. They want the strong
bodies of men who beat them and go to sleep afterward.

I feel the warm hand of one of the women on my arm
as she guides me into a seat. I would not mind standing
like I usually do, but it is nice the way the rumble of
the wheels suffuses my whole body. Sometimes, too, the
noise of the train is so loud that I get confused and lose
my sense of direction; although, even at the late hour
I travel, there are usually enough bodies to hold me in
place. This is the best time of the day, surrounded by
the warmth of human bodies and the smell of working
people, the lulling motion of the train. By the time we
get to Goudstadt Station, almost everybody is asleep,
comfortably resting against each other like a tangled
litter of kittens. The air is very close, but I never get
that feeling of being closed-in, surrounded, like I sometimes do in my elevator.

At the station now, I breathe deeply of the night air.
There is the lingering smell of exhaust fumes from the
motorcars, but still the air is purer than in the township. High heels clack cheerfully on the pavement and
there is the chatter of white people. They are going
home or are on their way to dinner in some lighted
restaurant. The women's voices whine, the men's are
suspicious, quick to turn to threat. Even when they
laugh, they sound guarded, as if they do not want to
say, ''Yes, it is me who is laughing.'' Only the white
policemen really laugh.

I walk the long way, past the park and through
Claim and Jeppe Streets. The other way is quicker, but
I am not in a hurry and I do not like to go past the
Beauty Shop. I can smell the burnt hair all the way
down the street. Sometimes along this way, I meet the
Indian vendor who will sell me the last of his day's *roti*
cheap. Tonight I am lucky. ''Here you are, my friend,''
he says to me in that funny singsong English, as if his

tongue is glued to his palate. "Vegibble roti. Very nice, very tasty." I bite off the crust and steam rises in my face, with it the flavor of many spices. I blow into the pocket formed by the pastry to tickle my nostrils again with the hot breath of cardamom, cumin, chili, coriander. I do not care if Constable Beukes tells me again as he did the last time, "Sies, man, you smell like a bladdy coolie shithouse." There are worse smells.

The chill given off by Hendrijkslied can be felt all the way over here, blocks away. The few whites in the area talk in hushed tones; my people hurry through. Except for those brave ones who are hoping to catch a glimpse of a lover or friend through the bars, no one wants to be near "the Place." My own steps are unchecked, firm . . . but I am careful to step around that patch of cold dark where Naroojian's body hit the pavement. His spirit sits here, now, waiting to touch the small of your back with fingers of ice.

I have no fear of the prison. I know its silent vaulted chambers. I know the dry smell of ancient evil in the former interrogation rooms in the old section. These now serve as offices for the bookkeepers and secretaries. I have scrubbed clean the rough edges of each brick in the stairwell, and my knees know each inch of floor that the Bosses walk on in their thick-soled, heavy boots.

Before old Gladkop taught me how to operate the lift mechanism, I traversed every centimeter of this building on my hands and knees, rag in hand, pushing before me the metal bucket with its acrid fumes of Lysol and greasy lukewarm water. Every night I tried to wash the floors and walls clean, but at the back of my throat there always lurked the salt reek of spilled blood, persisting through the astringent odor of industrial-strength detergent.

Gladkop rescued me from aching knees and a stiff back. He and I used to play Mrobaroba in the basement of the building. I would beat him too, since I remembered where every stone was placed on the worn leather board and would trap his men one by one. Gladkop got too old for his work and was going back to the kraal to live out his last days. He told me how he had watched me and was sure I could handle the elevator.

"You have to treat her gentle," he told me. "Listen to the motor. It has to purr all the time or she will shake and jerk when you stop." He told me that the bosses would get angry if the lift jolted them when it reached their floor, or if they stubbed their feet because it was not level. I did not disappoint him. I could feel by the give as I turned the heavy brass handle that the motor was pulling smoothly. The sound of the surrounding walls changes when you come to a floor, and I soon learned how long it took to move from one floor to another. The lift is like a huge and powerful beast that listens to my commands, and it responds best to gentle firmness. I like the pull on my stomach, chest, and legs as we go up, the lightness as we descend.

Van Tonder opens the iron gate that leads into the Place. "Another night," he says, bored. The door slams shut behind me. Van Tonder's weary steps shuffle to the stairwell, where he grinds another key into the lock. An electronic voice gibbers from his transistor earphone, where he is listening to a radio serial. Often he will tell me the wearisome, unlikely plots.

"These blokes had a helluva clever plan to rob a bank," he tells me now, standing with the metal door partly open. "They crawled through the sewer pipe until they were underneath the vault, then they broke in with hammers and picks. Foolproof. But one of these *ous* decides to smoke a cigarette while they're sitting with the loot, an' a old lady sees smoke coming out of the drain and calls the fire department. Is bloody bad luck, hey?"

Van Tonder is friendly for a policeman, almost kind,

but what a dull and tedious man he is! Talking with him always leaves me feeling as if all things in the world are equal and none of them matter much anyway. He leaves me alone now and I go downstairs to collect my bucket and mop. Skrik is sitting near the open elevator, smoking a cigarette hand-rolled with pipe tobacco. "Don't bother with that," he calls out to me. "It's been slow, so I cleaned already. But you may want to use some Brasso on the handle." Skrik is a prisoner on work duty. When his shift is up, he goes to Van Tonder to be locked up again in one of the common cells. He has been here for years, but I've never found out what he did. "Bring me mos some matches tomorrow, *asseblief*," he says as he's leaving. "The wooden ones. I'll pay you back." Wooden matches, the kind that will strike anywhere, are valuable currency inside. Skrik doesn't often ask a favor, so I will do what he wants.

The bell rings and I take the lift up to the tenth floor. Sergeant Van Wyk and a new constable with a young voice get in. Their breathing is heavy and they are sweating happily like rugby footballers after a game.

"You'll see," says Van Wyk. "He'll be ready to talk when we come back. The worst time for them is when we leave them alone afterward."

"Ag, man, you even scared me," says the younger man admiringly. " 'Here's your coffee,' you says, nice as pie. Then BOOM! you knock him right off his chair. Man, the look on his face—I just had to laugh."

"It's a matter of timing. Like telling a joke." Van Wyk's voice is even, his tone never varies. He likes to train the younger recruits, to be a father to them.

I let them off at the ground floor and they leave to wash up and have dinner. I remain waiting on the ground floor. Nothing happens, and the time passes slowly. Van Tonder walks by and tells me he is listening to "Death Touched My Shoulder." People send in stories to the radio about how they almost died. They get paid fifty rand if the story is used. Van Tonder has told me that if I can think up a good story he will send it in and we can share the money, but I can't think of any time I almost died that will sound like it happened to a white person.

I can hear distant singing coming from the rear of the building where the condemneds are kept. Someone is going to be hanged tomorrow, or maybe the next day. The condemneds don't sleep much and they sing all night: hymns, Zulu war songs, call-and-response songs about the doings that brought them where they are. Some of them have beautiful voices.

There is a dry rustling as one of the giant cockroaches that inhabit this building scuttles across the floor of the elevator. I have heard that one of the prisoners in solitary kept a roach as a pet and rigged up a miniature carriage for it, using his hair and a matchbox. Kobus Strijdom, *Captain* Strijdom, is mortally afraid of these insects although he is the most vicious of the policemen. Once, when I was taking him up to the tenth floor, he saw one of the roaches run up the side of the elevator. "Kill it," he screamed in a high voice that was not his own. Afterward, he was angry with me. "You bloody blind fool," he said. "Can't you keep the *verdompte* place clean?"

A "Black Maria" screeches to a halt outside. I regret thinking of Strijdom because now I seem to have conjured him up. The great iron gate clangs open and shut again and then a body crashes noisily against the side of the elevator. By the sound, it is not a very heavy body. Strijdom clumps in with his heavy boots, accompanied by an African policeman.

"Up, kaffir," he says to the figure in the corner. There are some more sounds as he and the African policeman get the figure to stand up. I turn the handle and start us ascending to the tenth floor, but partway up a strong hand yanks the handle back, jarring us to a stop between floors.

"We're going to make a little rest stop here, Stevie," Strijdom says hoarsely in my ear. He finds it funny to call me this, after Stevie Wonder. You can sense the violence in his very pores; he is always just on the edge of exploding. It is unbearably close in here with his hot, excited, sadistic smell.

"Tell us about your friends," he says tenderly. There is a sharp intake of breath from the figure but no cry of pain. It is a young girl. They have been bringing a lot of children here lately. "I'm not a patient man," Strijdom says, and again there is that intake of breath and the odor of fear overwhelms that of the captain's mad hatred. The child is brave, for there is again no cry, no begging for mercy. She is making a mistake, though; Strijdom will get what he wants.

"You think your lawyers are going to help you?" he screams, and says to the other policeman. "This one took me to court before. Mistreatment. 'Pliss, your honor, that policeman over there mistreated me.'"

There is a thud and a bang and the girl sobs quietly.

"This time you have a witness, kaffirtjie. Here's your witness." I can feel the child's face being pushed up against mine. Delicate fingers clutch at me for support . . . and swiftly insert a piece of paper into my pocket. The figure is withdrawn just as suddenly and there is a crash from the opposite side of the elevator.

"Ja," says the policeman. "Your mother can ask Stevie here what you looked like after I got through with you."

He shoves the handle roughly to resume our ascent. I bring the elevator to a smooth stop at the tenth floor and the three leave and go down the hall, the girl's feet scuffling against the floor as she is frog-walked between the two policemen. A door slams shut behind them and then there is silence. I do not wish to wait up here, so I take the elevator down again, feeling the tiny fold of paper crinkle as I lean forward. I go all the way to the basement and fetch a rag and a mop. The buzzer sounds, but I ignore it while I wipe off the sides of my cage, mop the damp spot on the floor. The buzzer rings again impatiently.

Van Wyk, Beukes, and the young constable are waiting on the first floor. "What took you so long, you monkey?" Beukes growls. He models himself on Strijdom, but he is just a bully, not a bottled-up spigot of acid. When he rides alone with me, he likes to snap punches that stop close to my skull. I act as if I do not know what he is doing.

"He's getting to be too lazy, *te vuil*," Beukes continues. "I don't think we should give him any of this tasty food."

The smell of Chinese food filled the elevator when they got in. Sometimes they bring food back for the long nights ahead of them or to frustrate a hungry prisoner by placing it just within his reach. I think of how even just not knowing whether to reach out for it must weaken resistance. Van Wyk hands me a cardboard box, greasy at the bottom.

"It's mos for you, man. Chow mein. A present, hey."

The box feels slightly warm in my hands. I wonder if they are playing a game with me.

"Thank you, my baas," I murmur.

"It's nice food," Beukes says expansively. "It's what the bosses eat."

I take them upstairs to the tenth floor and wait for a moment as the thudding of their boots recedes down the hallway. There is a sort of continual moaning sound coming from behind one of the doors. The long drawn-out moan follows me as I start back down to the basement and seems to linger in my ears after I know I cannot possibly hear it anymore. Downstairs, I raise the lid of the box and sniff at the mixture of meat, sodden bean sprouts, and soy sauce. I have eaten nothing but the roti all day and there is a hollow space at the pit of my stomach. I close the box and drop it in the rubbish bin, then I fetch my cold porridge and eat some of that. My mouth is very dry, so I wash down the pap with lukewarm water that tastes brassy from the ancient pipes. I have just finished my dinner when the buzzer sounds fretfully.

Beukes and the young constable get into the elevator on the tenth floor and tell me to hold it for the other bosses. They are chattering as excitedly as schoolchildren on their way to a picnic. I hear the slap of the leather holsters as they buckle on their belts, the click and drawing of bolts as they check their guns.

"Strijdom's good, 'strue's God," says Beukes. "Those buggers are going to be in for one hell of a surprise."

"Do you think they'll still be there?" asks the other policeman.

"Where're they going to go? Those mimeograph machines is heavy; you can't keep moving them around."

Strijdom and Van Wyk get into the lift and we start downward. There is again the snap of a shotgun breech, the clicking of shells. Strijdom laughs as he tells the others how I am going to be "a witness for the defense." He slaps me on the shoulder in a friendly way. His hand is solid and heavy as a steel bar. We reach the ground floor and the policemen leave the building talking in loud, assured voices, their rifles clacking aginst holstered pistols.

I ask Van Tonder for the stairway key, collect my supplies and take the lift to the tenth floor. I open the door to the stairwell and begin to sweep each step with unhurried strokes, working my way downward. I like this hollow, echoing chamber with its ancient stone walls. Their stubbly surface is cool and reassuringly

solid to the touch. In this silent vault, my thoughts run
free and I move as surefooted as a springbok on the
steps where handcuffed prisoners tumble into oblivion.
I listen to the whisking of my broom, stop and press
my knuckles against my eyes to see the bright lights
and colors.

I remove the piece of paper from my pocket, open it
and smooth it down. It is a slim, flimsy square that may
have come from a cigarette pack. I have no clue to its
contents. Probably it is just a name, a last shred of
identity. It is the girl's final cry: *this* is who I am, *here*
is where they've taken me. To have written anything
else would have been dangerous.

I don't know that I will show the paper to anyone.
Who could I show it to? Other prisoners have tried to
get me to run messages before and often I have been sure
it was a trap: Strijdom suspects everyone. I have no
wish to wind up in one of the rooms. Besides, Ma Thlaka
has warned me against talking about where I work. The
township youth have come to think that anyone who
works for a living is a traitor, and there are flames
waiting for those who associate with the hated police.

There is no helping the girl now. Her friends cannot
tear down these walls, and, besides, they will know soon
enough that she has been caught, too soon for them to
get away themselves. Her message is a message to me
alone, and I will hold on to it as I hold on to everything
else. Until the time comes. I carefully fold the paper
up again and put it inside my shirt pocket, against my
breast.

The long night drags on. I sweep slowly and rest
between floors to listen. At this hour, the springs of
time are taut enough to snap, each second a vast plain
that takes forever to traverse. I reach bottom, put away
my brush and pan and my little bucket of debris. I sit
down to wait for the bosses to come back with the day's
catch.

E X I L E S

This is how Mark comes to meet Zach' Mahlope.

A friend of Mark's calls him one morning and says: "Clarissa really likes you. Why don't you ask her out?" Clarissa is the friend's sister, a small dark-haired girl with a sidelong pickerel smile. Mark had found her attractive when they talked at a recent party but felt that he had not made a very good impression. The thought that the girl might want to see him again is cheering, but it is almost two weeks before he can bring himself to dial her number. There is no answer. The instant he hangs up, however, his own phone rings and it is Clarissa, who happens to be at a phone booth a block away from his apartment.

After an afternoon spent wandering around the West Village, followed by dinner at an inexpensive Vietnamese restaurant that they discover together, they find themselves in the Sunfish Café, the local bar that Mark often stops in late at night on his way home from the darkroom. Mark has been at low ebb, uneasy except in the company of a few close friends—although more than four months have now passed since his breakup with Kylie. He feels good now as he banters lightly with this pretty young woman, whose black hair seems almost blue in the dim barroom light and whose pupils merge into the dark irises. Clarissa is saved from conventional petite prettiness by a strong, almost masculine chin and that strange, sly smile.

"Stop looking at me that way," she says, dimpling. "You're embarrassing me."

"I was wondering how you photograph. . . ."

Fortunately this doesn't sound as stupid to her as it does to him, since she smiles at him with her eyes shuttered as she rises from the booth, saying, "I don't suppose this establishment has a ladies' room?"

He watches as she sidles past the bar stools toward the back room. It's not exactly the ideal place to bring a date, although the bar does attract a motley crowd of local workers, businessmen, and students. Nearby, the regular known as the Psycho Vet is holding forth in a loud voice. Mark had talked to him once when he sat on a neighboring stool at the bar counter, but he soon tired of the man's self-aggrandizing monologues and overt come-ons to any woman who passed within hearing range.

When he looks up again, Mark sees that Clarissa, who had stopped at the bar to order more drinks, is caught in conversation with the Psycho Vet and a black man wearing a peaked camouflage cap. Her head is tilted and he feels a rush of love at the vulnerability of her white nape, her neck as slim and strong as a gazelle's. Mark gets up and goes over to interpose himself between the P.V. and Clarissa. In the same moment, he realizes that he has midjudged the situation, for she is in fact happily looking at some photographs the black man has out on the counter.

"Cape Town," the man says. "My nephew sent them to me. Ag, they make me homesick."

Clarissa does not give Mark much chance to look at the photographs, but, pushing his drink at him, giggles: "Let's get drunk."

"Who's the South African guy?" Mark asked her.

"Jack. He's a custodian at NYU and he said he comes here just about every night. So you can talk to him another time. Right now, I've got dibs."

It is several days later before Mark again sets foot in the Sunfish Café. He has spent most of this time with Clarissa, and if anyone had asked how things were progressing with her, he would have had to reply: "Fast and slow." She stayed over at his apartment that first night, and each night since. They passed their time talking, making snacks, reading poetry aloud, and doing the *New York Times* crossword puzzle together, all punctuated by frequent hugging and caressing. It puzzles him that they have not made love, since it is clear they both want to. Mark wonders whether he has been trying too hard to avoid making the same mistakes he had made with Kylie. For in the process he has been making new mistakes: talking too much about his ex-love (a term which even now seems too harsh and final—he prefers to think of her as his "step-girlfriend") and there had been that awkward moment when Clarissa lifted one of his books out from the shelf and a note had fallen face up onto the bed. Kylie had been in the habit of secreting passionate letters to him all over the room. He thought he had found and filed away all of them, but apparently not ... and this one read:

"M.

> *I love you madly MAdly MADLY!!!*
>> *K."*

Signs of her, he realizes, are still all over the room. There is the box he keeps his bills in; it has her name and his address emblazoned on its side. There is the photograph of her over the kitchen table, the pair of women's shoes in his closet. . . .

Mark has forgotten about his compatriot in the bar until, coming back from the studio late one night, he notices the peaked cap sitting on top of some newspapers in the corner. He moves over to sit on the stool next to the papers and cap, just as their owner returns.

"Is your name Jack? My friend talked to you the other night. . . ."

"Zach'. Who's your friend?"

"Small, dark-haired girl? Clarissa. You were showing her some photographs."

"Oh, the chippie. You're a lucky bloke. What's your name?"

"Mark. I'm from Jo'burg. At least, I was born there. I haven't been back in a pretty long time."

Mark wonders whether he should have immediately mentioned his birthplace. You never could tell what the response would be, and he didn't want to have to go through the "My dad used to work for the Institute" routine to prove he was okay. The previous summer he had been wearing a University of Witwatersrand T-shirt sent to him by a friend, when he went out to buy detergent at two in the morning. As he was waiting for the light to change, a young black man leaned out of a car on the opposite side of the street and yelled: "Is you from WITS?" pronouncing the guttural Afrikaans W and flat I: "Vuhts."

"No, a friend gave me the shirt."

"I'm from South Africa, man," he shouted. "And I hate that fucking school. Don't wear that T-shirt, you understand!"

Before Mark could cross the street and talk to the man, the light changed and the car roared off, the driver calling out once more: "You musn't wear that shirt, hey?"

Mark had been surprised. Wits was the most liberal university in the country and the first to integrate—albeit the percentage of nonwhite students and lecturers had always been small. Mark's older sister had gone there, and he has always assumed that if he had stayed in the country he too would have gone to Wits, the spawning ground for progressive thinking among South African whites.

Zach', in contrast, is delighted by Mark's admission. "You're from Joey, 'ey? I'll drink to that."

He has obviously been drinking much of the evening and is in a mood to tell someone *all* about his life. Introductions are barely over when Zach' launches into his narrative, the only interruptions coming when he orders them both more to drink, or leans over to murmur conspiratorially: "You understand what I'm talking about. I've tried talking to this lot"—indicating the crowd around the bar—"but they don't understand fuck-all. In fact, they're always wanting to tell *me* about South Africa."

... I'm from the Western Cape originally, a little town named Underhillsrus. Our nickname for the place was Under-hell-we-rust, because it was a real dorp with no way out. But my pa was a Bible-thumper and he at least made sure I got a good mission school education. I never did get the calling, though; so after I got my matric' I went off to a technical college near Cape

Town. Olambane was a "mixed-race" techie, which
means that along with a lot of Coloureds they let a few
of us full-bloods in.

I did pretty well there and even had grand dreams
of becoming an office clerk, or maybe even a primary-
school teacher. Then two fateful things happened to
me: I took a course with Dickie LeGrand and I started
playing tennis. Dickie was a lecturer in sociology
who'd spent some time in America. The main thing I
learned from him was that it was possible for me to be
good friends with a white . . . even one who had the
power to fail me if he wanted. He not only didn't fail
me, but he got me to fight my natural laziness and send
out applications to study outside the country.

Tennis was where the real trouble started, I guess. I
used to do battle every day with Lenrie Stoffels on the
old cracked concrete squares that served as the school
tennis courts. To this day I have scars on my knees
from all the spills I took, but we got really good, I tell
you . . . so good nobody could touch us. In fact, we got
so good that we had the crazy idea of trying out for the
intercollegiate championships once we discovered that
there was nothing in the written rules to say a bush
college couldn't compete. It's just that nobody had
tried it before. All we needed was a letter from the
Registrar to state that we were students in good standing, which turned out to be no minor obstacle. The
Registrar was one of those craggy-faced Afrikaners
who look like they've been carved from a chunk of the
Drakensberg by an amateur. To complete the effect, he
wore a pair of oversize steel-rimmed glasses mended at
the rim with Scotch tape.

"You're asking me to stir up a wasps' nest, boys. Do
you realize that ?" he said to us.

"But, sir, all we want to do is play tennis," Stoffels
replied, as though the question had not been rhetorical.

The Registrar ignored him. "Let's think ahead a
little, yesss?" he said. "Suppose the teams from the
white colleges agree to play you, and you win . . . what
then? Do you really think anyone will let you play
Sterkfontein, or, God forbid, out of Cape Province al-
together? Of course most of the other teams will refuse
to play you."

"Under the rules, sir, they would forfeit . . ."

"No, no, my laddie. I simply can't allow you to bring
this kind of unwelcome attention—we're talking not
just about you but Olambane as well."

We were pretty downcast when we left his office, and
I was ready to give up right then. But not Stoffels.
Most of the time he was a playboy who didn't care
much about school and hardly had a thought for tomorrow, but once he got an idea in his head he stuck
with it.

"The man's talking shit out of his hat, yesss?" he
said. "I really don't give a damn if we get to play
tennis with a bunch of white boys or not, but I'm
bloody sick and tired of being told what I can do and
what I can't do. It's high time we stuck a firecracker
up the Registrar's arse."

Stoffels put all his energy into creating that firecracker: a petition to the school's Board of Chancellors. It started out with the simple request that we get
our letter, but once people started counting their grievances, they found a lot of them. Pretty soon the demands included an end to the seven o'clock curfew,
subsidized books for the poorer students (which meant
pretty much all of us), a course in "alternative" South
African history—i.e., one that did not revel in Boer
victories but told the story of how we had our land
stolen from us, a reprimand for any teacher who referred to his students as "this girl" or "that boy,"
and so on. We had five single-spaced foolscap pages by
the time we were done.

Stoffels wanted to be the one to present the petition, but Hendrickse, who had sat through the various meetings without saying a word, vetoed the idea. "Listen, Stoffels," he said. "There's no point your taking the petition to the Registrar. You're in scholastic trouble as it is. They'll just throw you out as a bad apple and forget the whole thing. But if Zach' and I present the petition..."

Of course, the university would have to take the grievances seriously if they were brought up by its two top students. Everyone had heard the rumor of how, only the other day, the Registrar had himself favorably mentioned Hendrickse's name at a meeting of the Chancellors.

He and I worked on the petition for a full day to tone it down, although there were still quite a few demands more than the tennis letter when it finally came time to hand it in to the Registrar. The response was swift. An emergency meeting of the Chancellors was called, and that same evening there was a knock at my door. The assistant to the Registrar stood outside, together with a burly white guy in a safari suit who smelled of police. They gave me a letter telling me that I'd been expelled for wanton and malicious conduct damaging to the best interest of Olambane College.

"Since you no longer have any reason to be in the area, you must immediately vacate the premises," the burly man said to me. He didn't give me any time to object but started pulling my clothes out of the closet and throwing them on the bed. I asked for some time to pack my things. He gave me one hour and told me he would wait outside the door until I was done. The worst thing was that only that very morning I had gotten a letter from Columbia University offering me a scholarship—providing I finished up the year in good stead.

I saw Hendrickse at the bus station ... climbing onto

a bus for Mafokeng or whatever little dorp he had sprung from. Stoffels I never saw again. One thing was clear: best student, worst student, it made no difference. They didn't give a damn about us; the only thing that counted was keeping your nose clean and your trap shut. . . .

Later that week, Mark takes Clarissa to his favorite photo gallery, which, coincidentally, is holding a retrospective exhibit of South African photography. Each photograph strikes him as remarkable, as if someone has developed the plates of memory in his own mind. There are pictures of men drinking out of milk cartons, lining up on the pavement to show their passes, or sleeping in crowded vans on the way to work. There is a late-nineteenth-century picture of Hottentots playing Ping-Pong in Johannesburg. There is the well-known picture of a black woman recoiling from the bared teeth of a snarling German shepherd—its leash loosely held by a policeman who himself is rushing forward with raised whip and gleaming boots.

Mark spends a long time in front of each photograph. Clarissa soon appears to grow bored, more interested in Mark than in the photographs. He speeds up his viewing of the exhibit with a mental note to come by again and see it on his own. Then he stops in front of a picture taken in the 1960s. A white child is leaning far out of the window of an old black Humber to touch the hand of a black boy of about the same age. The child in the car is ash blond and wearing slightly faded pajamas; the other boy is wearing ragged shorts that are a little too large for him. Mark recognizes the narrow, winding streets near the Jo'burg market, where Zulu vendors would whistle shrilly through the gaps in their front teeth as they pushed along heavy barrows filled with pimply, denuded chicken carcasses or great slabs of meat.

"What are you looking at?" Clarissa asks, edging close to him.

"I think it's me," he says.

... You asked me about Dickie. I was pretty dispirited when I arrived home, and my parents weren't exactly helpful: my getting expelled was a bitter blow to them as well, and they really couldn't understand why, in my father's words, I had been so stupid. I got a couple of messages from Dickie at the Indian grocer's, which at that time housed the town's principal telephone, but I didn't call him back. Then he and his wife stopped by to see me while they were on a driving holiday. I'm ashamed to say I was aloof, which I could tell hurt him ... but I just didn't want to be reminded of my failure. He kept telling me not to give up, to just make my way to America somehow or other. Once I was there, he said, no one would care whether I had finished up at the technical school or not.

Of course, there was a hitch—the authorities had their eye on me now, and after I applied for a passport I had regular visits from the local police sergeant. I won't bore you with the whole story, but there's one thing I still can't believe: that, even after everything, I thought they would just go ahead and give me my passport. It shows you how naive, how hopeful we still were in those days! I lost three months waiting to be told that permission was denied.

My next plan was to just get out of the country. I had heard that if I could get myself to Zambia, the ANC would help me get a plane to London and then I could get the Americans to help me from there. I sewed the letter into the lining of my jacket and got some false documents to show I was a migrant laborer from Malawi—no shortage of them! Someone got the wind up, though, and soon after we crossed into Rhodesia (this was before anyone had even thought of calling it

Zimbabwe), they pulled me and a couple of other blokes off the train. Whoever forged my documents didn't do a very good job, since even the thickheaded local cop recognized something was wrong—my picture had practically peeled away from its backing. The customs officer must have been asleep to let me through.

Well, they found the letter in my jacket and they assumed I must have hit this Zach' Mahlope guy on the head and stolen it from him. They kept me awake for three days—and me trying to prove the whole time that I hadn't killed my very own self! Then they hauled me in front of a D.O. who gave me six months hard for traveling with falsified documents. Man, I was shit-scared. I was eighteen, a little pretty boy, and I was stuck in some work camp in the bush with a bunch of common criminals. I'd heard about rapes and stuff . . . how if you're young they make you the woman and everybody has his turn.

My first night in the prison hut, I was trembling all over trying not to look scared. There was this ugly older guy with a beard and one eye missing who kept looking at me. I thought I'd had it when he came over to me. "You from South?" he says. He was a political, from PAC. You know about the Pan African Congress, right? Hector Makhulo was his name, and he saved my skin. Once the crims saw I was with him, they didn't look at me again. There were a couple of rival gangs in there, and the leader of one of them got interested in the political education Hector was giving me. It was unnerving, the way these hoods would squat silently on their heels listening to us talk about means of production and the rise of the working class.

Hector had been in a lot tougher places than Malopindi Corrections Center. He'd even been on the Island where he'd gotten to wave to Sobukwe and Mandela.

"Just stay out of the hands of Lynus Van Niekerk,"
he told me. We'd all heard about Van Niekerk: who
liked to boast that he knew his prisoners better than
their wives ever would. In fact, the only time I ever
saw Hector look uncomfortable was when I asked if the
rumors about the policeman were true and what that
meant. He wouldn't answer, but just kept saying I had
better get away before I ran the risk of finding out for
myself. I knew I owed my survival at Malopindi to
him, and I even started to dread the end of my prison
stretch when I was to be deported back to S.A.

The day before I was released, Hector gave me the
names of some PAC people in Gaberone and one final
piece of advice. "When the train stops in Botswana,
get up and walk out the door. I don't think they have
any jurisdiction there."

I somehow kept my cool until we pulled into Gaber-
one, where I told the South African cop who was ac-
companying me that I needed to take a leak. He didn't
even look up from his newspaper. I walked out the door
like I knew exactly where I was going and, man, I just
kept on going. Hec had made a smart guess. None of
the countries involved wanted to go through extradi-
tion hearings; they simply relied on us to be good boys
and sit quietly while we were carried back into the
Republic. You know, Hector had a favorite saying: "A
whipped dog doesn't know when its collar is off. . . ."

Crossing the street one day, after he has dropped off
Clarissa at her Chelsea apartment, Mark is almost run
down by a familiar figure. It is Serge, his former roommate, recognizable anywhere by his question-mark
shape: slight build, head hunched down, stomach
thrust forward and shoulders and hips back. Serge is
thirty-five but looks older; an Armenian refugee from
Bulgaria, he is working as an intern in a lab at NYU

while he studies for his medical boards. He is a self-proclaimed expert in "adaptogenics"—drugs made from plants, such as Siberian ginseng and Schizandria, that are claimed to bolster the immune system. Serge was forever consuming pills of hard-packed vegetable matter and vials of evil-smelling liquid, but to little effect on his habitual jitteriness.

"I must eat *quickly*," Serge used to reply to his roommate's suggestion that he sit down to eat his dinner of Chef Boyardee or takeout lo mein. On weekend nights, Mark would come home late to find Serge lying in the dark on the living-room couch. Mark would be preparing a 2:00 A.M. snack in a last-ditch attempt to avoid the next day's hangover, when he would suddenly realize that there was a still but quite conscious and sentient body on the couch in the unlit living room. After a while he grew to expect, and even dread, this lonely nocturnal presence.

"Tell me something nice," Serge would say, heaving a deep sigh. Mark would describe the course of his day —the classes he had gone to, the customers who showed up at the processing lab, the friends he met in the evening, the movies he saw. "That's nice," Serge would interject periodically.

"Serge, how are things?" Mark now asks, pleased to see his former friend. Serge shrugs: What can one expect? " ... And your father, is he still living with you?"

Mark had finally decided it was time to seek a new place to live when Serge's elderly father, a widower who was a slightly smaller replica of his son and had the same question-mark shape, moved in with them "temporally." Father and son would have long debates in Armenian at the kitchen table. Once in a while, Serge would reach into his pocket and absentmindedly put a cigarette into his mouth; the old man would just as absentmindedly lean over and slap it to the floor before Serge had a chance to light it. Mark had been able to gauge the length of their conversation by the number of broken filter-tipped cigarettes lying in a half-circle around the table.

"He is still living with me. It is very bad. He said he would go out if I bring woman home, but where would he go?"

"What about your exams? And your paper . . . did you get it published?"

Serge had shown Mark the paper he was writing on plant pharmaceuticals. Serge's supervisor at NYU had told him to redo it, since the bulk of the paper consisted of lengthy quotes by various experts, followed by brief interpolations: *Dr. X of Y University writes . . . In disagreeing, Dr. Z. responds . . .*

"Terrible. All terrible. I am always writing, I am always studying." The answer comes forth in a spate of words, followed by a dramatic pause: "But I never give up. If I gave up, I would still be in Bulgaria."

Mark recalls with a blush how, when his finances were horrible and he was not sure if he would be able to pay the rent on his studio, he would cheer himself up by saying these very words.

"You're still in Bulgaria," Kylie had yelled at him one day.

It is Saturday night, and Mark, who has been unable to reach Clarissa all day, calls up his friend Gary to see if he has any plans. Gary, who knows Mark from California, invites him to a party that turns out to be held in a run-down building on Manhattan Avenue and 110th Street, a neighborhood marginal enough to make Mark wary of walking there at night. Gary, however, is very much part of the New York scene and never seems to much care what part of Manhattan he goes to or what comments and strange looks are elicited by his long blond ponytail. Mark's nervousness increases with the trouble they have finding the address because the numbers on most of the buildings have been totally or partially erased, but at last they find the right place. Mark notices that the lock to the front door is broken. Through the grease-smudged glass panes he can see the figures of two black men loitering in the lobby.

"I think we should wait a minute..."

"What for?" Gary asks, pushing his way into the building. "Come on, I think it's on the sixth floor."

The men in the lobby follow them silently with their eyes as they start up the unlit stairway. Mark feels his back muscles tighten and he only relaxes when he can at last hear music and see light filtering through the doorjamb of their destination. Later in the evening, he sees one of the men from the lobby again: the hostess, a short, attractive woman wearing a low-cut blouse, is hand-feeding him an empanada.

... I managed to find my way to the American Embassy with no trouble, and I called up the numbers Hector had given me. That was the easy part. The embassy wasn't sure whether I would be traveling to the United States as a student or a refugee; they kept telling me it would be easier if I had travel documents. I wound up sitting on my thumbs for six months, bored beyond words, before I was able to make all the arrangements to come here. If it wasn't for the PAC people, I would probably still be in Botswana while the embassy made up its mind. Then, when I got to this country, I called Columbia and they told me that my scholarship had been given to someone else because they hadn't heard from me.

I worked for PAC for about six months, going around the country giving lectures to various colleges about the evils of Apartheid. I started getting really fed up with the whole thing. Kids would always ask me

*if I'd been tortured; then they'd seem disappointed
when I said no. It made me think of Hector, and I
wondered how he'd feel if he became a professional
exile on parade. You tell the same story over and over
again, and after a while it becomes unreal. Finally I
just packed it in. Needless to say: my friends at PAC
were pretty angry. They called me a petit bourgeois, a
traitor to the struggle, the whole thing. But I just
couldn't face one more college student asking me: "So,
how does it feel to be free?"*

Mark is taking an advanced course in photography
at Hunter College. He loves the hours in the darkroom
—the sulfuric acid smell of the developer and the magical way an image would form on the white paper,
spreading from the middle outward, rapidly, like some
instant Shroud of Turin. He loves the warm red,
womblike glow, the intimacy he forms with a girl who
always wears the same fuzzy mohair sweater and seems
to share his schedule. They often brush against each
other as they move from the enlarging lamp to the
chemicals, but to speak would break their bond.

The people in his class think Mark's black-and-white
photographs of New York were taken in Johannesburg.
One picture shows a bare-chested black man carrying
a rolled-up carpet on his shoulders. Back-lit by bright
sunlight, he looms enormous, his burden larger than
himself. In another picture, a bearded and tangle-
haired tramp gives the viewer a gap-toothed grin as he
proffers an unlabeled fifth of some grain spirit. It is
not only the subject matter that seems imported
straight from South Africa. In the quality of the light,
in the angles of shadows falling from abandoned buildings, in the stance and posture of the human parade,
the camera chooses to fix those moments that mirror
the lost reality of a distant land.

. . .

Mark calls Clarissa to see if she wants to go with him to Zach's fortieth birthday party. She tells him no; she is going to watch a baseball game with a friend in Brooklyn.

"This is your chance to see a bunch of South Africans get roaring drunk," Mark cajoles. "How can you pass up such an opportunity?"

"I can't miss the Mets! You know, the season's just started and I even went out and bought myself a cap to watch the game in."

"Another time, then?" Maybe when the season's over.

"Mmmh."

When Mark arrives at the party everyone else is already there, excitedly watching the game on a small black-and-white TV in the living room. He helps himself to a beer in the kitchen, then wanders over to the couch on the far end of the room to read an old copy of *Staffrider* that he found on a bookshelf. A young woman sits curled in an armchair nearby, her attention taken up by a sleepy cat that tolerates her caresses with mild ill temper. Her hair is long and straight and hangs down to hide her face as she leans forward to pet the cat; now and then the scrim parts to reveal large, pretty eyes and skin pitted with acne. Mark's thoughts turn sadly to Clarissa, who is probably sitting before a wide-screen in some Brooklyn bar—everybody's darling in her Mets cap, with a stein of beer clutched in her small fists.

"Is that a South African magazine?" the girl asks, awkwardly looking away from Mark.

"It's a literary magazine that I think's folded. The name comes from young African daredevils who would run along the roofs of moving trains."

She looks puzzled, so Mark adds, "Westerns are very

popular in the township. The guy who rides on top of the wagon is said to be riding staff.''

''Oh, I'll have to ask Simon if he ever did that.''

The latter turns out to be her boyfriend, Simon Nxhlenge, a tall wiry fellow who is sitting directly in front of the television cheering on the Mets. ''Soccer was always my game,'' he later tells Mark. ''But I love watching baseball. There's this moment when the batsman looks in the pitcher's face and tries to figure out what he's going to throw. It's like when you're in a bar and you notice that some tough is looking at you. You don't know whether he's going to pull a knife or buy you a drink.'' He mimics the staring-down, the uncertainty on the victim's face.

Simon reveals that he is studying journalism through Columbia's General Studies program. His inspiration is Nat Nakasa, the young black journalist who founded *The Classic,* an important literary magazine in the sixties.

''I met him when I was a little kid. We gave him a ride to Durban,'' Mark reminisces. Nat was unlike any adult he had met before, keeping the children entertained with absurd jokes about parliamentarians and pumpkins and the difficulty of distinguishing between the two. Mark remembers Nat's ''proof'' for transmigration of the soul—that dogs understand Afrikaans. ''If a dog hears me speaking Zulu, he'll run after me and bite me; but if I shout *voetsek* at him in Afrikaans, he will run away. You see, if an Afrikaner is very good in this life, then he gets reborn as a dog. But if a dog behaves badly, he has to come back as an Afrikaner.''

''You met Nat? Whites have all the luck.''

''He was a great guy. I can't believe he committed suicide.''

''He didn't. He was pushed,'' Simon says with conviction. ''The police had to kill him because he was too dangerous to be allowed to stay alive.''

Simon returns to his seat in front of the television and Mark watches the screen from the back of the room. He tries to see it the way Simon does, but all he can discern are distant stick figures moving back and forth and the occasional close-up of a strong jaw vigorously chewing gum. His head feels heavy with beer, and he is relieved when Zach'—whom he did not notice leaving the house—reappears with several family-size buckets of Kentucky Fried Chicken. Someone else has bought two more cases of beer, and they all watch the Mets, gnaw on chicken bones, and drink from bottles that are icy from being in the freezer. Near Mark, a Xhosa named Johan and a Zulu named Solly are disparaging each other's tribal leaders with mock ferocity.

''That Matanzima, he put his own brother in jail. His own brother!''

''And Buth'? His brother picked up some white dollie in Sun City and moved her into the ancestral kraal.''

''You'll be sorry when Buth' is running the country.''

''Everyone will be sorry....''

The drinking continues unabated after the game is over. Mark knows he has reached his limit, though he is unable to resist taking another near-frozen bottle when the Mozambiquan whose name he has forgotten hands it to him with the words: ''In my country, we call beer like this 'stupid with cold.' '' There is a ring at the front door, followed by a loud banging in the hallway as a tall youth comes in tripping over his guitar case. He is dressed in jeans and denim jacket, has a remarkably friendly grin and long red hair braided into dreadlocks. His guitar case is plastered with stickers bearing the symbols of countries and towns—the

Eiffel Tower, Copenhagen's Mermaid, elephants rampant from some indeterminate African game park.

"It's Julian," Zach' and Johan shout simultaneously. "Come on in, you Boer!"

"Zach', Johan, Solly, Si," Julian beams. Simon nods imperceptibly, intent on picking at the label of his Brahma beer, which has begun to separate from the bottle as moisture condenses underneath it. "Julian Visser," the redhead introduces himself, extending his hand toward Mark and in the process almost kicking over the low coffee table.

"He's an Afrikaner, but I had to teach him Afrikaans," Zach' roars, while Julian looks happily around him as if not knowing Afrikaans is an accomplishment.

"My mother is English," the youth explains. "Her and us kids staged a coup in our household—no Afrikaans. I almost didn't get my matric' because of it."

"The only songs Julian knew were bloody rubbish by Jackson Browne and Billy Joel," Zach' grins. "So I taught him 'Suikerbossie' and 'Sarie Marais'—"

"And 'Daar Kom die Ali Bama...'"

"Ja, but I'm not talking about the slave songs, I'm talking about the real *Rock* songs, the ones the old boer Rocks sing when they sit around the braai after a hard day of kicking kaffirs out in the fields."

"Zach' means my father," Julian responds. "He's a real *verkrampte,* a hard-liner. He couldn't believe it when he came to visit me and finds I'm sharing a flat with a black man."

"His dad walked in when we were all sitting around singing Afrikaans songs. He didn't know whether to shit or cry or just be happy that his son is finally learning *die taal.*"

"O bring my terug na die ou Transvaal," Julian sings in a voice that is hoarse and untrained yet pleasant to the ear.

"Very touching," Simon cuts in. "If we can just get

Botha and Mandela to sing 'Sarie Marais' together, we could forget Apartheid and all live happily ever after."

There is an embarrassed silence, broken at last by Zach' saying in slightly aggrieved tones: "Simon takes things too seriously. You can't hate a language; especially since it's us Coloureds who invented it ... though I'll bet you the government would like to hang me for state terrorism for even suggesting that idea."

"I don't care if I never hear another word of Afrikaans in my life," Simon mutters.

"You spend too much time worrying about women," Zach' tells Mark when they are sitting in the Sunfish some weeks later. "You can't rely on someone else to give meaning to your life, you have to do it for yourself."

"What are you suggesting in their place? Drinking?" Annoyed, Mark almost adds *"Social activism?"* but thinks better of it.

"No ... I suppose I'm jealous. Your obsessions are at least normal, the sign of a healthy ego. I can look at a pretty woman and feel attracted to her. I can lie all night in my bed and fantasize about her, or worry about why she rejected me, or just think of the nice time we might have had. But I can never forget who I am, that I am this displaced person with no roots and no reason for being here except that I can't go home. Sometimes I walk along the pavement and I feel it all slip away from me. I become disembodied, and I have to tell myself not to ignore the cars when I cross the street."

Zach's speech—which has the ring of something said or thought often—dispels what's left of Mark's irritability. "I don't know," he responds. "You seem to serve as a pretty solid peg for some people. Like Julian."

Zach' smiles. "Julian's a child, a naïf. He even tells me I'm his *true* father, as if you can choose to take on new parents. You know, he pitched up in New York with just his guitar and a little money, no plans."

"And he found his way to you."

"Ja, I was looking for a roommate and this bloke I know who deals with draft resistance passed him on to me." Zach' paused and smiled in remembrance. "A couple of months after he came here, Julian got busted in Penn Station with a bag of pot in his jacket pocket. He was high as a kite, picking over and over at the same chord on his guitar. I had one hell of a time stopping him from being deported, I can tell you that. We had to get half the bigwigs in Harlem to testify to his good character . . . and that includes this preacher I know. We told the judge, this boy left his country because he didn't want to fight against his black brothers. He's heartsick over the horrible things going on over there. That's why he smokes pot."

"The real reason we left South Africa," Charles Spiegelman used to tell the English and American guests to their London home, "was *not* that I had to witness the filthy hands of an Afrikaner policeman going through my wife's underwear. *Nor* that my principal achievement seemed to be in helping hitherto mildly discontented Africans educate themselves to the point where their only possible response to their own impotence was to become hopeless drunkards, outcasts in both the white world and their own. *Nor* even that I myself had to compromise my ideals every day so that I could keep the Institute open and be praised for my idealism. *But* that I did not want to see my sons grow up and be inducted into the South African army."

While this argument was invariably well received by their visitors, it was a constant source of annoyance to the adolescent Mark, who wondered why he had not

been consulted in a decision that had been taken for his
"own good." Charles was the only one in the family
who truly found the move to England a positive one.
Mark's impression was that his father's work was a
pleasant round of reviewing grant proposals from al-
truistic researchers wishing to study the infinite range
of ills brought on by racism, punctuated by the business lunches at the inner city's finer restaurants, whose
details he would later recount at the dinner table. For
the children, England was characterized by its oppres-
sive crampedness. They had moved from the beginning
of a South African summer into London at midwinter,
and the large but dingy apartment and dull gray days
made Mark long for a country that took on greater
brightness with its ever-increasing distance.

Mark and Joel had been accepted into a prestigious
high school run on public school lines; its headmaster
had a habit of waiving the school's rigid entrance re-
quirements for foreign children, taking the neo-Dar-
winist view that there must be some spark of
intelligence in anyone whose parents had the good
sense to leave their blighted countries for Blessed Al-
bion. The rich blue of the school uniform announced to
the world that the wearer was a member of the intellec-
tual elite and made Mark and Joel's walk home
through a rough neighborhood of poorer local schools
even more perilous. After one particularly harassed
journey home through a chilling mist of fine rain,
Mark railed at his father: "You're always talking
about how we left South Africa to gain freedom. Here,
I'm afraid to go outside half the time. *I* was much freer
there."

"What ever happened to Simon?" Mark asks Zach'
one day, when they are once again bellying up at the
Sunfish. "He seemed like a nice guy."

Zach' gives him an ironical look. "Simon? *Nice?* There's nothing 'nice' about Simon."

"Interesting, then."

Zach' heaves a sigh, then replies: "That interesting, nice guy broke his sweet little girlfriend's jaw a couple of weeks ago. He used to beat her up something terrible —I can't tell you why. Maybe because she was white and rich and pretty and thought she loved him. Maybe because he just enjoyed doing it. Julian told me the story. I wanted to kill Simon ... or at least knock some sense into him."

"What happened to the girl?"

"Oh, I don't know. She spent a night or two in the hospital and then they let her go. Her parents were plenty upset: I heard they got the police after him, but she persuaded them to drop the complaint. If he ever goes near her again, he'll be in big trouble—I can tell you that, boy."

"Is anyone in touch with him? He seemed so smart ... even if he was angry."

"Actually, I did see him. Yesterday, in fact. He was sitting in one of those needle parks on Seventh Avenue yelling things at nobody. Just another crazy black man in New York City. I walked past him a couple of times but he didn't recognize me. Finally he looked up and said: 'You got a brother? He just walked by.'"

Although he senses it is a lost cause, Mark calls Clarissa several times, until she agrees to meet him in the evening after one of her summer classes in philosophy at Columbia. Her sister had already told Mark that Clarissa has three passions in life: men, Kierkegaard, and baseball ("or baseball, Kierkegaard, and men— the order varies"). She had also intimated that Mark has blown it, though she did not tell him this outright.

As Mark rides the No. 1 train up to Columbia, he

reviews in his head all he plans to say to Clarissa when he sees her: that she should know he was simply distracted by his own confusion and not indifferent to her, that it is a misjudgment of the situation not to realize he *does* care for her, that they should give it another go.

He leaves the 116th Street station and walks over to the Columbia steps still muttering to himself his incontrovertible arguments. Although he is late for their rendezvous, she is later still and he seats himself beside the statue named Alma Mater to wait. A couple comes out of the Philosophy Building and stand in close conversation for a minute or two, then the girl detaches herself and hurries toward Mark with quick, light steps.

"Clarissa!" he calls out as she is about to walk past him.

"Hi. How are you?" Her face is set as if there is some task she feels she has to get through.

"I'm okay," he replies. "What do you feel like doing? It's such a nice night, maybe we should just take a walk?"

She shrugs assent and they start strolling back toward Broadway. Mark realizes that there is no point in saying any of his rehearsed thoughts, and he wishes he could just cancel out the evening and be back in his room with a book and his music, or in the Sunfish with Zach'. By the time they have bought ice-cream cones at Häagen Dazs and sauntered back onto campus, they have both thawed enough to be enjoying each other's company. Clarissa even laughs when he reads aloud some of the names carved above the library: "Demosthenes. Plato. Aristotle. I didn't realize the alumni were quite so famous."

They go and sit down in a grassy lot that is generally filled with sunbathing students during the daytime but is now quite empty. It is a perfect early summer night.

The air is warm, but not uncomfortably so, and there is a floating diaphanous mist that lends a mood of magical unreality to the surroundings. Mark likes listening to Clarissa's half-humorous ragging on her classmates' pettinesses and stupidities—it is her "lovable brat" quality—and is glad now that they met here and not in some noisy anonymous bar. As he glances around, though, his eye is stopped by a ghostly movement in the grass some distance away. Peering harder into the surrounding darkness, he notices several more faint gray shapes moving around the lawn.

"Let's go," he says quietly. He stands up and holds out his hand to help Clarissa up.

"But it's so nice right here . . ." she says.

"Seriously, I think we should go."

They begin walking toward the nearest opening in the fence and still she has not noticed the gray shapes. But just as they step onto the path, a large rat dashes squeaking in front of them as it heads for shelter in the bushes.

"Ugh," Clarissa says, and suddenly shivers. "I hate those things. No matter how long I live in the city, I'll never get used to them."

"They're all over the lawn. They must have been hiding in their holes when we first walked in."

As if to herald the irrevocable breaking of their pleasant mood, a speaker in a nearby dorm blares out some very loud and indistinguishable heavy metal music.

"Do you ever feel," Mark muses, "as if you had slipped just a little bit out of time, maybe taken a right turn where you should have taken a left or gone back to check whether you'd turned off the light in your room when what you should have done is left the apartment right away . . . and now everything is just that little bit out of kilter and you'll never quite catch up?"

"No."

. . .

Mark has just finished working a half day at the
photo lab and is about to head home when he sees Zach'
coming toward him. Zach' is on his way to visit a mu-
sician friend of his and he invites Mark to accompany
him. As they walk, Zach' mentions a program on poor
Afrikaners that he has just seen.

"I used to hate Afrikaners before I came to this
country," he says, "but from this distance I can finally
have some grudging sympathy for them. Not for the
government, of course, but for the ordinary, everyday
worker who's terrified that someone of my complexion
is going to steal his job. When I heard this woman
talking about having to queue up to get milk for her
kids, I felt such a rush of nostalgia. She sounded like
my mother."

"It's funny, as an English speaker I was probably
more insulated from Afrikaners than you, or even most
Africans. We never really dealt with them except when
we went on holiday and drove through small towns. In
fact, for a lot of my friends, their first encounter with
living with Afrikaners was in the army . . . which can't
be the best way to get to know a people."

"Ja, from here you can see how much my culture
and theirs have bled into each other." Zach' grins. "I
guess I just miss what was familiar. If I ever went
back, my sentimentality probably wouldn't last a
day."

They stop to buy falafel at a Lebanese shop and go
into a park just off Avenue A to eat their sandwiches.
The park is deserted except for a few tramps sleeping
on the benches and the ubiquitous drug dealers indifferently murmuring "Smoke? Smoke?" Mark initially
feels nervous sitting there on the pigeon-fouled bench
away from the bustle of the streets, but Zach's calm is
contagious as he holds forth on his friend's musician-

ship ("He plays too much George Benson stuff, but
his tone is outstanding").

They leave the park and walk down the far side of
Avenue A, past a fenced-in construction site. A group
of lean and muscled black teenagers are hanging about
the fence, occasionally tossing a stone or can into the
gaping hole left by the ground movers. One of them
looks hard at Mark and Zach' and whispers to his companion. Zach' pays no attention and continues talking,
but just when they seem safely past the gang, Mark
detects a movement behind him. An arm snakes around
his neck and he feels the sharp point of a knife blade
pushed up against the base of his ear. He stands absolutely still while expert hands go through his pockets.
Behind him there is the sound of scuffling feet and he
hears Zach's voice, "Come on, brothers. We're not rich
folk."

Mark starts to turn around, but the arm tightens
around his throat and a quiet, firm voice behind his ear
says, "Just be cool." There is a thump as something
solid hits human flesh. The arm around his throat is
suddenly withdrawn and Mark is given a shove that
sends him staggering into the fence. Turning, he sees
their assailants start to run off, but one of them stops
and kicks hard at the head of the prostrate figure on
the sidewalk. Once. Twice.

"I hate these fucking Africans," the youth says, before he too pivots and runs away. "They're always
giving you shit."

Mark arrives at the hospital, where after two and a
half days Zach' has just regained full consciousness.
He has a subdural hematoma and is still having trouble
with one of his eyes. When Mark walks in, Zach' has
his eyes shut and Julian is asleep on the armchair
where he has been sitting for the past forty-eight hours

picking over and over again at the chords to "Sarie Marais." He has somehow charmed the nurses into letting him stay—despite his dirty bare feet that protrude from beneath his curled-up legs.

Zach' wakes up with a start. He takes a moment to regain focus before he recognizes Mark, who is relieved when Zach' smiles and it is clear he does not resent Mark's escaping unscathed.

"I'm glad he's asleep." He indicates Julian fondly. "He was beginning to drive me crazy with his boere songs."

"I'm told it's good medicine," Mark replies.

"I'm sure. The worst thing is I'm not allowed to laugh, or to cough. I can feel this tickle deep down inside me, but I have to suppress it." He closes his eyes and is silent for a few minutes, then he murmurs, "The real worst thing is that I only had about ten dollars on me. I have no idea what I was fighting for."

SERVANT PROBLEMS

Paul was sure that he had put the ten-rand note in his trouser pocket the night before, yet it was no longer there. Every Sunday morning he was up early and at the Johannesburg Market by seven-thirty. He had already wasted half an hour looking for the money, which he had specifically set aside to buy fruit.

"Why don't you have some breakfast, love, and then go to the market," Alisse said. "There'll still be time to buy apples and oranges, and those are really the things the kids like best anyway."

He went to the market for the children. Their healthy, sun-browned bodies were proof that the move back to South Africa from London had been the right one. He had hoped to buy them papayas today, as the season was just starting, but it was too late for that now. The Afrikaner retailers would have already grabbed up the best fruit. It was annoying; he had been looking forward to seeing the kids' faces when they tasted "pawpaws" for the first time.

"I want to see Daddy," a sleepy four-year-old's voice sounded from the passageway alongside the bedroom.

"No, Michael, Daddy's cross."

"With me, Mommy?"

"Not with you, little one. Daddy's lost some money."

Her jocular tone, as if dealing with an idiot's mood, was unpleasant to him. Well, it was better not to get upset. He would go and eat breakfast and the servant could pick up the clothes that lay strewn around the room.

"Florence!" he shouted.

He could see it so clearly. Early in the morning when she brought in the tea—with her foolish smile and nasal "Mawning, master. Mawning, missis"—she had turned her back on them to straighten out the clothes on the chair. That's when her quick hands went through his pockets for a little unofficial bonus.

"Master?" came the anxious call from the kitchen. He waited for a few minutes, but the servant did not come.

"Florence!" he called, louder this time.

"What, master?"

"Don't stand there in the kitchen shouting. Come when I call you."

Florence waddled quickly in. She was fat, rolls of merry black fat with a gap-toothed grin—the archetypal African mama whose bulk hardly fit through the doorway. She was nervous now and sweat began to trace small rivulets down her plump cheeks. Her mouth was set in a sullen pout.

"Florence, I am missing ten rand. I put it in my pocket last night . . . and now it's gone." He realized his words sounded harsh, but, for some reason, the clean pink of the uniform with its peeping fringe of lace petticoat, its widening stains of sweat, combined to particularly infuriate him.

"Master! I am an honest woman," she began to shout at him. "I wek hard for you and never take nothing. You always leaving money around, maybe your children take it. I wek before in a big house with lots of nice things and I never take nothing!"

"I'm not accusing you, Florence. I just wanted to know if you had seen the money."

"Well, master, I haven't seen it." With a last baleful glance around the room, she returned to her kitchen still muttering about the fine house that she used to work in. Only the week before, a former maidservant had returned to see if there was any work for her and Florence had run outside and said: "I'm wekking here now. You can go away!" Now she considered the place beneath her station.

Paul went into the dining room and sat down. He picked up a muffin, broke it in half to expose the steamy white interior, and began methodically to put butter and jam on it. The jam was homemade and it tasted delicious.

"Daddy, please don't be cross," Michael said.

"I'm not cross," Paul said, leaning over to ruffle the child's soft brown hair. As he did so, he felt the ominous crinkling of paper in his shirt pocket.

"I've found the money," he exclaimed. "Let's call in the Flod and I'll tell her."

"Shhh! She'll hear you."

The Flod, a black flood of a woman, came into the sun-filled dining room. She was carrying a tray containing a fresh batch of hot muffins.

"I've got the money, Florence, just as I thought. You see I wasn't accusing you."

Florence, seeming little appeased by his admission,

continued to cluck and sigh under her breath. "I tol'
you I never tek nothing."

"You see, honey, there was nothing to get angry
about," Alisse said, to his instant annoyance.

"You know I have to put up with all sorts of crap at
work. The least you could do is take care of things at
home."

"What are you talking about? It was your idea to
come back to this bloody country, and now *you* don't
want to be aggravated."

This outburst was too much for Paul and he stormed
out of the house, leaving her angrily tearful and the
children confused. He sped the little red Austin down
the driveway, in reverse. A crackle beneath the left
front wheel signaled the end of some plastic toy that
one of the kids must have left in the driveway. It only
served to exasperate him further. The toy ought to
have been picked up by one of the servants.

He drove along the road, down the hill and past the
ugly construction site that was ruining the scenery of
the old suburb, until he came to the Melrose Bird Sanctuary. He began to walk inside the sanctuary but returned hurriedly to the car. He was not in a mood
simply to enjoy the area's beauty, and, besides, he had
neither bird book nor binoculars with him.

As he climbed back into the driver's seat, he noticed
a bundle of clothes behind him. They belonged to that
damn African, Wilson. Wilson had begun his job as
garden boy with a frenzy of activity, digging fervently
among the flower beds with a trowel. His principal
accomplishment had been to kill a number of perfectly
healthy plants by exposing their roots. Then he had
come to Paul and told him, "My father is very, very
sick, baas. I must go back to the kraal to see him." He
had borrowed some money against his salary and never
returned, but he had left all his clothes neatly folded

in a cardboard box in the garage. Paul intended to take the African's clothes to the house where he had originally picked the man up. He did not want to take the bundle to the police, who would probably have arrested Wilson for no longer having a valid passbook.

Paul now drove to the house where the African had said his sister worked. A large black woman was walking down the driveway, a milk bottle firmly clutched in the crook of her stout, pink-overalled arm.

"Hey," Paul said. "Is your brother here?"

"My brother, master?"

"Yes. The fellow who used to work here—Wilson."

"Wilson? He just work here. He not my brother, he a Malawi." She paused, and announced proudly, "I am a Tsonga."

"But he *told* me you were his sister."

"That boy! Heh! What he done?"

As she obviously did not know of Wilson's whereabouts, and Paul did not share her amusement, he thanked her and drove off. His anger was now weary and defeated. He remembered laughing contemptuously with Alisse about a conversation at his aunt's house. His aunt had invited over some young people to meet the newly returned couple, and conversation had revolved around white Johannesburg's pet topic: servant problems.

"Never trust a Malawi," his aunt had said ... and repeated.

He drove around the suburbs of Benoni, taking some pleasure in his skill at down-shifting at the turns but none in the pleasant, lush, but well-tended gardens. Stopped at a traffic light, he noticed ahead of him a tall African talking to one of the prevalent black "nannies" in a bus shelter. The man was waving his hands theatrically, and the woman was showing her white teeth and rocking from side to side in appreciation.

"You are too funny," she shrilled, just as Paul stopped, unnoticed, a little way ahead of them.

"Wilson!" he shouted.

The African looked around nervously but could not see where his name was issuing from.

"Wilson!" Paul shouted again.

The black man came running over to the car, his eyes enlarged and showing white with fear. He was trembling and he looked dazed.

"Master?" he murmured, his voice not assured as before but not undramatic.

"Ah, Wilson. I knew I would find you here. Now I want you to take your clothes out of the car and give me back the money you owe me."

Paul leaned over and opened the back door to allow the African to remove the box. He was relaxed and unhurried, almost as if he had arranged a rendezvous with Wilson on this very street corner.

"Master, I have no money," said the African after he had taken his clothes out of the car.

"Now listen here, Wilson. You come and break my plants and run away with my money, and then you say you have none to repay me with. What kind of show is this? Hmmm? I knew where to find you and I know you are lying when you say you've got no money."

"No, master, what I say is true." And to prove his point, Wilson began to throw the contents of his greatcoat onto the street as if this ritual would appease Paul's anger. Letters, paper clips, delivery notes, rags, and a soiled white handkerchief formed a small pile next to the car.

"No, Wilson, I cannot take a man's money if he says he has not got any. That is, if he *is* a man."

"I am a man, master."

"Well, if you are a man, you will bring me my money when you get some. If you are not a man, if you are a little child, then you will not honor your debts."

Paul started to drive homeward, smiling. Wilson owed him a small sum, and it would not really matter if he never got it back. In the distance, he could see a roadside stand where some small black children were selling fruit; it would be only slightly more expensive than the market.

"I am a man," the African said, frenziedly throwing the last of his property onto the dusty street.

A SOWETO EDUCATION

Some months before the school closed, the teachers at St. Joseph's attended a staff meeting where the issue of the politicals was raised for the first time. Lately, there had been disturbing signs of restlessness among the students, and on everyone's mind was the recent incident at the government school in Moroka township, where rocks had been thrown and tear gas had invaded the playground.

There, was, of course, little fear of anything on that order happening here. As St. Joseph's headmaster was fond of saying, he ran a tight ship—an admission that had earned him the name "Principal Ahab" from the geography teacher. It was this small but plucky man who had brought up the matter, his eyeglasses misting with nervous heat as he appealed to the headmaster: "Mr. Johnson, we cannot simply shut our eyes. We must have a policy, answers...."

The headmaster, a heavyset, pale-skinned man with thick, puffy cheeks that gave him an air of contained truculence, leaned forward, his chair creaking beneath him, and said: "There will always be lazy, vulgar boys who like to be disruptive. Send them to me and I will deal with them."

Mr. Johnson let his full weight bear on the table and paused to examine his large, liver-spotted hands. He looked up, glanced slowly around the room as if seeking out disruptive elements, and continued: "Any troublemakers shall be treated with the greatest of severity. The very *uttermost* severity."

"But what is it they want?" Miss Winston demanded crossly.

"I suppose they want us to teach them how to throw stones and petrol bombs," Teacher Morena replied. "As if you can get your matric' by throwing stones." He noticed that the attractive Miss Tlinga was looking at him with approval and continued, "We have to make them understand that it is only through learning that you can make your life better."

It was almost dusk when Teacher Morena left the St. Joseph's school to begin his walk home. The sky was a soft pastel blue and the clouds were lightly streaked with ocher. Teacher strolled easily along his familiar route, his briefcase in one hand, his tan raincoat folded and grasped in the other. He felt tired but relaxed, and his mind was filled with a pleasant tangle of ideas, bits of the day's lessons, disembodied quotes from his reading, and items from the Latin he was teaching himself in the evenings. *Sum, esse, fui.* I am, to be, I was. A language of great poetry, "the father of our own tongue." He remembered how one of his tutors for the teaching certificate, Mr. Mulcahy, liked to stress the importance of the classics. "Never forget that the edifices of today rest upon the bones of the dead," he would declare.

Teacher barely looked at the familiar jumble of township housing, boxes with corrugated iron roofs and smoke rising from the yard; hardly smelled the stew of odors rising from the discarded "Kaffir beer" cartons, human sewage, and assorted rubbish; took no notice of the children darting like scavenging dogs between houses or sitting with their feet in the warm runnels of muddy water on the side of the road—the road with its ridged spine and miniature chasms that chewed the innards of the few hardy cars and trucks that bounced their way in and out of the township. His thoughts were on the future, when a tidal wave of progress in the form of a line of bulldozers would clear away the matchstick houses, and then housing projects with electric light and running water would spring up in their wake. The Future, Progress, Education... these were the ideas, palpable as meat and bread, that he sought to pass on to his charges at St. Joseph's.

Teacher entered the house from the side door that opened into the passage leading straight to his room. He did not need to light the kerosene lamp that Ma Nhlovu had hung for him on the hook just inside the doorway, and which he now picked up to carry with him into his room. He knew every step along the way, had walked it so many times in the five years he had lived in the boardinghouse that he could walk it in the pitch dark and not stumble. He was the only boarder now, though at one time there had been several: a laborer who smelled of cement dust and sweat, a young woman whose numerous small children would knock pleading at the bathroom door while Teacher familiarized himself for the final time with the day's lesson plans. Ma Nhlovu's heart had increasingly given her trouble, and when the other boarders moved out she

did not try to replace them. She had had enough of
overseeing a crowded household and now divided her
time between taking care of Teacher's small needs and
hosting her ladies' nights. It was said that Ma, a short,
wide-hipped woman who always wore a *doekie* to cover
her coarse, close-cropped hair ("so the mens should not
see the gray") had once been a famous shebeen queen
before she was stricken with "heart." The only remaining evidence that supported this rumor was the
way she liked to sweeten her teapot with lashings of
ginger or peach brandy on the nights other like-aged,
like-minded women came to her house to play cards
and sing hymns.

Teacher carefully set the lamp down on the workbench that also served as his desk, turning his head
away from the strong odor of kerosene that filled the
room as he took off the glass chimney. As he was trim-
ming the wick, he realized, startled, that there was
someone else present in the darkness behind him.

"Easy there, man," a hushed voice spoke to him
urgently from the far corner of the room. "There's
nothing to worry about. It's just me, Langa."

"What are you doing here? How did you get here?"

"My driver brought me," Langa said sardonically,
then laughed. "Aren't you going to ask me how I am,
Titcha-boy?"

Teacher did not reply. He struck a match and lit the
lamp, then turned the flame down low to keep the chimney from cracking as it warmed up—soothing himself
with the familiar gestures. Langa was his cousin; in
fact, they had grown up together, although they had
not seen one another since they were twelve or thirteen.
Teacher had heard various conflicting reports about
Langa's activities over the years: that he had joined
a gang of *tsotsis*, that he was in jail or on a work farm,

that he had been stabbed in a knife fight over a woman. For a long time now, Teacher had heard nothing of his cousin at all.

There was a knock at the door and Ma Nhlovu, swaying heavily on her feet, came in with two steaming bowls of maize-meal porridge and meat. She placed both bowls on the workbench and asked: "You are well, Teacher?"

"I am well, Ma."

She glanced up at him, said "I too am well," and went out again, her soft closing of the door shutting out the sound of women's voices that had drifted in with her. Ma Nhlovu had made no acknowledgment of Langa's presence, her eyes never once straying in the direction of the corner where he sat, and were it not for the second bowl of food, Teacher would have been convinced she did not know there was a stranger in the room.

Teacher brought one of the bowls over to Langa, placed the kerosene lamp between them, and sat down. They ate quickly and in silence, and while they ate Teacher took the opportunity to study his cousin. Langa was darker-skinned and a little shorter than Teacher himself but just as thin. However, his was a wiry slimness betokening strength. Teacher noted a narrow, crescent-shaped scar just above Langa's left cheek and thought: "In a crowd, I would not have known him."

When he was finished, Langa pushed the food bowl to one side and began to rearrange the burlap sack he had brought with him and which he was using to prop himself up. The sack made a metallic noise as it was shifted, causing Teacher to wonder whether it contained tools of trade or pots and pans to set up house.

"Tell me, Langa," he said, "are you looking for a job in the city?"

"It does not matter what I am doing. I am not even here." The flickering lantern gave his face a satyric look. "Your woman there, the one who brought us food, she knows I am not here. You should be wise, like her."

Teacher said nothing. In childhood too, he recollected, Langa had been given to sudden outbursts of anger or would go for days in sullen silence, a smile as of some superior knowledge occasionally playing across his moody features. In those days, Teacher's mother worked as a cook in a house in Turffontein and was lucky enough to be allowed by her employer to have her children live with her in the servants' quarters. She had pretended to the mistress of the house that Langa was her eldest son, and he had lived with them for about a year while his own mother looked for work in the city.

His mother was busy caring for her employer's family during the day, so Teacher (who then went by his given name of Jakob) and Langa spent most of their time alone together or with his mother's friend, a watchman for a nearby clothing store. Part of the watchman's duties were to tend to a large German shepherd that guarded the alley behind the shop against thieves who might otherwise break in through the back window. The watchman introduced the boys to the dog, showed them how he fed it, and warned them not to get too close when he was not there.

Langa and Teacher often used to play behind the wood fence in the back of the alley and watch the dog. It was a large morose beast, the black saddle of hair on its back almost obliterated by the dust it liked to roll around in. The dog spent most of its day sleeping, but it moved with surprising speed and agility whenever someone stepped into the entrance of the alley. It would launch itself forward with a low snarl and hurtle toward the intruder, only to be pulled up short a few feet from the entryway by the length of thick rope attached to its collar. The boys would delight in the way unwitting passersby would shriek and drop their belongings as the dog rushed toward them.

One day, the two boys were sitting on top of the fence enjoying the warmth of the afternoon sun and idly seeing who could flick a pebble farthest. They noticed a small but well-fed cat coming down the alley toward them. The cat sat down in a patch of sunlight and began to leisurely lick itself clean. They could hear the dog growling deep in its throat as it prepared to attack, and Teacher wished he could somehow warn the cat but he was unable to think of a way to do so in time. The German shepherd bounded toward its victim, but was yanked backward a few feet before it reached its target. Again and again it charged, each time being pulled up short by the rope. The cat watched imperturbably, unmoving.

Langa suddenly leaped down from the fence and began to throw stones at the cat, calling it a variety of filthy names. The animal gave him an indignant look, rose, and without seeming to hurry, moved swiftly out of the alley.

"That bastard, Jakob. That blooming bastard! Did you see how he sat there with his nose in the air like madam waiting for her tea? I'd like to see Skapie tear him up. I'd like to see Skapie catch him and tear him up."

The following day the cat was there again, and again the German shepherd tried in vain to get at it. Langa did not interfere this time but sat on the fencepost watching coldly, occasionally muttering to himself.

On the morning of the next day, Langa asked the old watchman if he could feed the dog. The man agreed, warning him to be careful not to get bitten. Once the boys were out of his sight, however, Langa handed the dog's feeding bowl to Teacher.

"Here, you feed Skapie. Just keep him away from me for a minute, okay?"

Teacher was nervous about feeding the dog, but it followed him docilely when it saw he was carrying its food. Langa, meanwhile, removed a piece of rope from under his shirt, cut the dog's leash at its base and tied a rapid series of knots to join the two pieces of rope so that the dog was still prevented from escaping but now had an extra nine or ten feet of leeway. This accomplished, the pair were about to climb to safety again when Langa abruptly grabbed Teacher by the back of the neck and thrust him hard against the fence.

"You don't try nothing stupid, you understand?" he demanded, pushing Teacher's face against the rough wood.

They sat on the fence for several hours, waiting. Once, Teacher suggested that they go home and see if his mother had any cake left over from the afternoon tea, but Langa curtly told him to shut up. Then they saw it, the gray and white cat, daintily walking into the alley. It lay down in its usual spot and began its cleaning ritual; Teacher could see the long pink tongue wash methodically over its paws. Somewhere at his feet the low growling commenced as the dog worked itself into a frustrated rage. Teacher almost cried out but was stopped by an angry look from Langa. The German shepherd rose and charged, its stride lengthening with each bound, and it was going at top speed when it hit the cat, the two animals rolling over and over in the dust together. Separated, they looked at each other in surprise. The dog was the first to react, seizing the cat by the scruff of the neck and whipping it from side to side so rapidly they seemed to merge into a single blur. Teacher watched with the astonished unbelief of a spectator to a motor accident as the cat was reduced to a mat of bone and hair, a trampled wig. Behind him, the air was filled with Langa's wild laughter.

. . .

Teacher returned from school the following day to find Langa in much the same position he had left him. Again they ate dinner in silence, and again Langa, by his general demeanor, discouraged any after-dinner conversation. Teacher marked papers for a time and then looked at his Latin primer, though he found it difficult to concentrate. Glancing over at Langa once in a while, he saw that his cousin was also reading something: a battered, leather- or cloth-covered object too thin to be a book, too thick to be a pamphlet. Langa's intense concentration suggested that he was reading a religious text. Finally, unable to contain his curiosity, Teacher asked: "What are you reading?"

Langa, who seemed unusually relaxed, quickly grew expansive. "This is an *American* book, called *How to Be Successful*. Listen: 'Success is dependent on desire. You have to want success so badly that you eat success, sleep success, walk and talk success, even brush your teeth in the morning success! Unless you put your whole heart and soul into it, you will never attain the success you want and so richly deserve. You will remain one of the many might-have-beens.' "

Langa read with the slow, halting speech of Teacher's schoolboy students but when he began speaking again, his eyes seemed to bore into Teacher's and his voice was hypnotic.

"You see, Jakob, nothing can be gotten unless you truly want it. We who have nothing, have nothing because we never demand what we want. We have even become ashamed of our wanting. But all that is going to change. Yes, as surely as I am here it is going to change!"

"You want to get rich?" Teacher inquired, uncertain where his cousin's speech was leading.

"Au, you understand nothing. You!" Langa spat in

disgust. Angrily he took up his book again and began to rifle through the pages, making it clear that the conversation was over.

Then, some time later, he asked: "What do *you* want, Teacher?"

"I? I do not know. No, that is not right. What I want is to teach, to impart knowledge. And then there is a woman, Miss Tlinga, who is another teacher at my school. I am thinking that sometime soon we should get married. I have been saving some money to put down on one of those new government houses for our children to grow up in. I would like children—not right away, but I would like them."

Teacher was too engrossed in this vision to notice that Langa had grown steadily angrier and angrier.

"Oh, how nice," Langa burst out. "How awfully jolly, how jollyfine. You are like a bug in the wall. *Sies*, man, a stinkbug. You come out and sit in a little patch of sun and you say 'How good my life is! How jollyfine.' Then, one day, a *man* will notice you as he passes by, and . . ." Langa made an ugly gesture with his thumb.

On subsequent evenings the two spoke to each other hardly at all. Langa stayed in much the same position the whole time: on the floor, his back resting on the burlap sack, his eyes on the door; but he seemed not so much to be idle as to be waiting with restless immobility for some distant signal. Teacher was relieved when he returned on a Tuesday evening a little over a week after his cousin had first appeared and found that Langa had gone as swiftly and unexpectedly as he had come. Teacher had come to the conclusion that his cousin was mentally unbalanced. Madness was not a new thing to the township; in fact, it lurked around every corner for those too unwary to combat it, striking most often at those who were unemployed or had lost their jobs and spent their listless days drinking in the shebeens, ever fearful of passing patrols. There was the Mad Muslim, who handed out joss sticks to passersby and beat his forehead on the dusty ground, oblivious to the shouts and comments of the people around him. There was the toothless old woman on Koornhof Street who would wait for the men to pass by on their way to and from work and would leer at them, raising her skirts high in the air. Like them, Langa was mad. The mad millionaire! Teacher regretted mentioning his savings; he felt lucky that he had not been asked for money.

"This is terrible, really terrible," the geography teacher said. "Those freedom fighters make me sick."

The staff room was crowded as it usually was early on a Thursday morning, with all the teachers getting ready for class or having a last cup of coffee before the day's work began. There was a pause in the bustle; the diminutive geography teacher had a way of voicing what was on everyone's mind . . . and consequently outraging *somebody*. He sat now, sunk deep in the large armchair with his feet resting on the magazine-littered coffee table before him, his face obscured by the back-page portrait of a handsome smiling man advertising Lucky Strike cigarettes.

"What does that mean anyway?" he asked. "Freedom fighters? That they fight freedom?"

"That they fight *for* freedom," said Miss Winston, who taught grammar to the Standard Sixes. Realizing that this might be taken to signify approval, she added, "At least, that is what the term means."

"Listen: 'Terrorists sprayed the downtown Johannesburg OK Bazaars with automatic rifle fire early yesterday morning. Some twelve people were killed and another fifteen seriously injured before police, who rushed to the scene, were able to subdue the terrorists. . . .' '' He clucked his disapprobation. "Mmm, mmm . . . Oh yes, this they had to throw in too. 'Among the wounded were several of the black salesgirls whose hiring caused considerable controversy several years ago. *They will be compensated fairly, like our regular employees,* the manager of the OK Bazaars announced at a press conference. . . .' They never stop, I tell you, they never bloody well stop !''

Around midmorning, one of the students interrupted that day's lesson on the uses of pronouns to say that the school should close early to honor the dead or captured freedom fighters.

"We should close early to mourn for those innocent people who were murdered by savages,'' Teacher stormed.

He ordered the class to join him in five minutes of silent prayer for the victims. Looking around the room through half-shut eyelids, he saw that only a few of his pupils had followed his example; the rest scribbled in their notepads, slapped surreptitiously at each other, even sat bolt upright staring defiantly at him. He realized that, for the first time since he was a young student-teacher, he had lost control of his class.

When class resumed after lunch, Teacher discovered that a number of the students had stolen away, had taken it upon themselves to leave early that day. Many of the others had somehow gotten hold of strips of black cloth and were wearing them as armbands. The class was calm, nonetheless, and the students seemed attentive to their lessons.

At the end of what had been a long and tiring day, Teacher returned to the staff room to have a cup of tea and relax before going home. He opened the newspaper that lay carelessly discarded on the coffee table, and read : "Of the five terrorists, three were killed in their battle with security forces and two were captured. The two were identified as Langa Mondhlane and Jackson 'the Knife' Kogasana. 'We have been looking for this pair for a long time,' a security police spokesman told reporters. The desperate gang are believed to have entered the Republic from Mozambique. . . ."

He had not known that fear could strike with such physical impact, that he would grow dizzy with shock in the way one grows dizzy if he looks down while crossing a narrow footbridge, his field of vision closing in as though the universe were suddenly contracting around him. The teacup rattled on the saucer he was holding, bringing him back to reality as he half placed, half dropped it back onto the coffee table. The sound also alerted the geography teacher who had just then walked into the staff room.

"What is the matter, Mr. Morena?" the other man asked. "You are not ill, I hope."

"It is nothing, just a passing chill."

"You must take care of yourself. There is a bad flu making the rounds."

Yes, it did feel as if he were in the grip of a fever. Ice seemed to clutch at his bowels at the same instant as his face flushed with heat; drops of perspiration sprung up at the hairline and ran with cold clarity down the back of his neck.

The geography teacher offered to assist him home, but Teacher refused. (A brief vision of policemen at the school gate, the geography teacher arrested as an accomplice.) There wasn't anyone waiting for him at the gate, but the way home was not easy all the same. The ground seemed to float beneath Teacher's feet; he could not focus more than five or ten feet in front of him, and his peripheral vision had disappeared entirely. Often, he had to pause, trembling at the knees and out of breath, and rest against a wall or lamppost for support. His thoughts were completely taken up with the business of getting himself home, yet he noticed that the streets were more than usually crowded, that many of the people hurrying past him, shouting as they went, wore the ominous black armbands.

Back in his room at last, Teacher lay for hours in a semistupor devoid of thought, the fear still a physical affliction. He slept; his sleep was marred by visions: a dog thundering down on an unmoving and uncomprehending cat, Langa making over and over again the same brutal gesture with his thumb. Late in the night, Teacher was awakened by sirens, shouts, the sound of running feet, but these things seemed not to have to do with him, for they soon passed off into the distance. Still, his ears strained for the expected heavy footfalls, the terse knock on the door. He had no doubt that Langa would take pleasure in revealing his innocent complicity; perhaps his cousin would even convince the police that Teacher maintained a regular harbor for passing terrorists.

He wondered if he should go to the police before they came to him, should confess his guiltlessness before he was unjustly incriminated. But why should they believe him? It would simply be a matter of hastening the inevitable, of stepping into the lion's den. He could not forget the unpleasant encounter with the police that had taken place just the previous year. He had been returning from a multiracial convention of teachers at Witwatersrand University when he was suddenly plucked from the crowd by a strong hand at his shoulder.

"*Waar's jou pas, jong?*" a stocky white policeman with a smooth, bland face and an ash-sprinkling of a mustache demanded of him.

"I'm a Coloured. I'm not required to carry a pass," Teacher had explained, but the man guffawed into his face, revealing yellowed, carious teeth.

"You think you're the first kaffir to try to fool me with that line? Fanie," he called to a huge Zulu policeman standing close by, "stick this boy in with the rest of those dumb bastards."

Teacher broke away from the Zulu, who had begun pushing him toward a waiting police van, and said: "Please, there's been a misunderstanding."

Something silver glinted at the corner of his eye and he made the mistake of turning toward it instead of away. The enormous, shambling Zulu had wrapped a pair of handcuffs around his fist and he struck Teacher on the temple, lifted him contemptuously off the ground with one hand, and threw him into the van.

Teacher had been bailed out early the following morning by a lawyer sent by his headmaster. A fellow educator had seen the incident and reported it to the school.

"You really should carry some identification; then mistakes like this wouldn't happen," grumbled the desk sergeant who was returning Teacher's belongings. Noticing the cut above Teacher's left eye, he said: "What happened? You fall down the stairs?"

"Yes," the lawyer said quickly. "He slipped."

The policeman nodded judiciously. "Accidents will happen, you know; you've got to watch your step."

Once they were outside again, the lawyer had said: "No sense looking for trouble, is there?"

"I was just unlucky, I guess," Teacher had responded, wanting only to get as far away from there as possible.

Teacher woke up the following morning with a high fever and all the signs of a severe viral infection. He made his way to the kitchen, where he asked Ma to dispatch the news to his school—through any passing schoolboy—that he was too ill to come in that day. Back in his room, he was surprised to feel how weak his legs were and it took considerable effort for him just to rummage through the cupboard for extra blankets. He knew it would look better if he did not interrupt his teaching schedule, but he was too ill to care. He lay in the bed with the blankets up to his chin, but he was still so cold, so cold, and he imagined that the chill that bit into his very marrow came from the cement of a cell floor, that the ache in his feverish bones was the tingling aftermath of kicks and blows, that the moment was just a brief respite before the next round of beatings.

In the afternoon, he had visitors. The geography teacher, his small eyes gleaming anxiously behind round spectacles, told him that the school had closed early because of the riots all over the township. "I told them that there was going to be big trouble ahead," he said, sounding pleased with his prophetic powers as he sat squat-legged on the corner of Teacher's bed. Jenny Tlinga, who arrived as the geography teacher was leaving, sat primly on Teacher's desk chair with her legs crossed. She brought sweet orange cake and further news of the troubles within and outside the school.

Teacher was glad of the distraction of company, but he worried that his friends would be implicated with him, and he was further made ill at ease by the impossibility of voicing his concern. It was conceivable that his house was already under observation and note being taken of all who passed through its doors. With that single uncaring stroke in his choice of a place to stay, Langa had destroyed Teacher's life. Not just his life, but all he had ever stood for. The school itself—which headmaster Johnson liked to refer to as "the

Eton of Soweto''—would be viewed with mistrust, a spiderweb of suspicion radiating out from Teacher to anyone who had contact with him. His own solitariness and hardworking scholarship would now be seen as clandestine activity by a fugitive and secret plotter of insurrection; the worst students, those who blamed the world for their own shortcomings, would take heart from what they would believe to have been Teacher's role. He saw now how easy it was to make a mockery of a man's life, to overturn his dreams and leave him with nothing.

The days passed, and Teacher's fever slowly abated. The drone of helicopters, disrupting his diurnal nightmares, heralded the quelling of the riots, and the midweek newspapers reported that the township was quiet once again. Teacher followed the course of the freedom fighters' trial with the avidity of a child following a comic strip serial and received his information in the same halting and repetitive way *(the story thus far . . . the new development)*. Much was made of the presiding judge's declared intention to have the trial proceed as speedily as possible ''to demonstrate that, in this country, justice is prompt and swift.'' A map of the terrorists' presumptive route was presented and Teacher saw with some relief that they had the dates wrong. It was reported that the police, who had set up roadblocks at random, had captured several armed men hiding in a delivery truck bringing sides of beef into the city, and the reporter speculated that the OK Bazaars attackers had very likely used a similar ruse.

It began to be clear to Teacher that Langa had not, as yet, betrayed him. He wondered if he was being toyed with, if he was being allowed to build up hope only to have it rescinded at the last moment. He thought often of his cousin at the hands of the police, who he knew would not be gentle, given the offense. But then Langa was like a marathon runner who sees the finishing line a few yards ahead of him and so is immune to pain, to the pelting of the elements against his already bruised body. No, he resembled even more one of those terrible swift *spruits,* the destructive streams that sometimes appear after a violent summer downpour and rush across the open veld smashing everything in their path . . . leaving here and there a bridge intact, perhaps with its supports gone so it would collapse at the weight of a child or an old man. He did not need Teacher's pity. For Langa, the things that were not part of his singleminded destiny were unimportant to him and so dismissed out of hand. Pity, pain, the questions of the police : these were all peripheral to him, outside of his consciousness, and therefore unable to touch him.

Teacher returned to school and found it all strange and disquieting, as if he were viewing himself and others from a great height. It was only his automatic familiarity with the school routine that kept him intact that first day. Several times, though, he lost his train of thought and stood silent for a moment or two until he remembered where he was. ''My nerves are shot,'' he told himself, ''but I must keep calm and continue as if nothing has happened.'' The strain made him prone to jump at the slightest noise, and his students, quick to sense weakness, became increasingly rowdy and disobedient.

Returning home that same day, Teacher read in the evening newspaper that the two terrorists had been found guilty. Because of the politically sensitive nature of the trial, the press had been forbidden access to the courtroom during the defendants' speeches. Now they were invited back to hear the judge solemnly intone to Langa and Jackson the Knife: "You will be hanged by the neck until you are dead."

The date was set for the Monday morning a week later, and Teacher was shocked at the enormous sense of reprieve this gave him. He would not really be safe until Langa was dead and their secret buried with him. But that *he*, who had never wished harm to anyone, should long so vehemently for his cousin's death!

It was late on Sunday night after a near sleepless week. Teacher sat on the rough wooden lid of the toilet in his tiny bathroom, the Latin primer in his hand. *Sum, esse, fui.* It would not be long before it was dawn and Langa would be hanged, which was very likely no more than he had expected, or wanted. Teacher tried to conjure up an image of his cousin but could only come up with a picture of a callused thumb thrust violently downward. He wondered why Langa had never betrayed him. Under torture, it is said, men will reveal things even they had long forgotten and surely a name that Langa had only contempt and derision for would be the first to pass his lips? *Amabo, amabis* ... I will love you, you will ... He fell asleep, the riddle unsolved.

Teacher woke as the first light crept in through the dusty grate high above his head. He stood on the wooden seat and peered out of the barred opening high on the wall, seeing the pasteboard houses of the township as stark in the early morning light as figures in a charcoal engraving executed by a madman. He started suddenly, his foot nudging the book which fell to the ground with a soft thud. Far in the east, the city was on fire! Teacher stared blankly as the blaze grew and spread outward; he continued to stare long after the rapidly rising orb of the sun had alerted him to his mistake.

T H E   M A N   W H O   S A T

At first slowly, then imperceptibly faster, then fast, the droplet of water sloughs downwards, following the wet, filmy track of its predecessor. Stopped at a bend in the trail, it is in turn engulfed by the gravid, oblongate globe that has rushed down on it from above. Now, a new trail has been created for each arriving drop to follow ... drops that beat with increasing steadiness against the windowpane.

Panos Demitopoulos sat placidly on his hard wooden chair, a chair that had grown comfortable with long use. He paid little heed to the outside world, where rivers of water red with mud gushed from the arterial gutters of the suburb like warm earth's blood. For him, it was just a faint blur beyond the window, the grumbling of thunder and sudden fire-flash of lightning, dull and distant occurrences forever outside of the

warm room ensconcing him. There was no one there to
wonder at his uncomprehending gaze or at the stoic
stillness with which he occupied his rough throne behind the counter. After all, there was nothing in his
little shop so indispensable as to entice someone to
brave the fierce storm that was vengefully playing itself out on the cracked streets and shabby houses. Nor
did Panos note the absence of his fellow man, for he
was brooding on the circumstances which had left him
to this lonely indolence.

Panos's principal memory of his early years was of
the occasions that his mother would pull him to her,
squeezing his round cheeks with her plump, callused
hands as she marveled at his talents. "The only one of
you with any brains," she would announce to the dis-
pleasure of his older siblings—who would taunt him
with his "superior intelligence" when he said or did
something foolish. He did not know of a particular
reason that his mother had singled him out, but he
accepted her conviction of a finer destiny in store for
him, her last-born. He once won a prize for handwrit-
ing, but then, what child does not win a prize for something? However, he would often think of the prize and
the joy it had brought him and his mother, and he
would wonder to himself when the next mark of high
favor would occur and what form it would take.

Panos's big chance did not come until the year 1960,
when he was twenty-five. He had settled into a pleasant
if largely inactive life of working as a seasonal waiter
at the single large hotel on his home island of Mykonos.
The rest of his time he would spend lingering idly at
the outdoor tavernas or occasionally ferrying an off-
season tourist around the island in his brother's taxi.
He had learned a little English and a smattering of
German, had grown slightly thick-bellied, and was neither particularly satisfied with his lot nor discontent.

He knew that at some point he would have to find a more stable means of income, but jobs were scarce on the island, and for now, he was willing to let things remain as they were.

Panos was resting in the shade of the vine-covered arbor at the front of his brother the taxi-driver's house, having shared a lunch of plump quail that his brother had shot that morning, when he noticed a distant figure in a black dress moving up the rock-strewn path toward them. It was his mother, and he idly puzzled over what could bring her out in the midday heat.

"What is it, Mama?" his brother Nikos called out, having also noticed her arrival.

Their mother said nothing, fanning herself with a white-and-blue envelope while she caught her breath. She seemed unusually excited, and one strand of silvery hair had slipped from its restraining wimple and was plastered across her forehead with perspiration.

"It's Konstantin," she gasped, pulling a crumpled note out of the envelope. "For Panos."

The only Konstantin he knew was the ferry-master, and Panos could not imagine why the man should be trying to contact him, especially by this novel means.

"My brother, Konstantin. Your uncle in South Africa," his mother continued, seeing the puzzlement on his face. She handed him the letter which contained the terse and ironic message: "I have the spitting disease. I will die soon. Send the smart one to take over my grocery. K." This was followed by an address written in the unfamiliar letters of the English alphabet and accompanied by a money order for five hundred South African pounds.

He had all but forgotten about his mother's brother, who had emigrated when Panos was still an infant, but evidently Uncle Konstantin had not forgotten about him. Now Panos wondered why his uncle had decided to impose this journey on him, when the money could have been usefully spent to start up a perfectly serviceable grocery right here on the island. He made this suggestion to his mother, who grew uncharacteristically angry.

"That is not what the money is for. My brother is ill and has sent you this money so that you can relieve him of the work in his shop. It would be wrong to use it for any other purpose."

"This is your chance to get rich," Nikos chimed in enthusiastically. "If Konstantin can send you this much money, think how much more he must have attached to his shop. You can spend a few years working hard, then you could come back here and settle down. Just think of all the young women on this island who'd be only too happy to marry a rich man!"

Panos wished that his father were still alive so he could ask his advice. He could remember how, on the few occasions Konstantin's name was mentioned or a letter arrived from him, his father would give a derisive snort and say: "So, when is he going to send us some of those diamonds he was always talking about?" Panos had little wish to go off to a distant land he knew nothing of, despite the enthusiasm of his mother, brothers, and sisters and all their talks of "opportunity, gold, and diamonds."

"What's keeping you here?" his brother Nikos demanded.

When a friend who worked regularly at the hotel told Panos that it was unlikely they would be hiring extra people this season, he took it as a sign that his fate was sealed.

Panos was fortunate enough to be able to book a berth on a Greek freighter that kept a few passenger cabins available for members of the shipping company. The fare was much less than that of a regular passenger ship, and he was pleased to note that he would have several hundred pounds left over when he got to Cape Town. During the first few days on board the Greek boat, Panos was seasick and felt confined by the ship's limitations, but he soon found life aboard not to be drastically different from that on Mykonos. He got on well with the crew, who were predominantly Greeks from small islands and whose view of the world was much the same as Panos's own. His time was taken up in sleeping in the shade of the quarterdeck, chatting with the sailors about the simplest ways of fishing and making wine, or drinking ouzo and playing cards with the ship steward (who confessed in a carefree moment that the ouzo was paid for by Panos's fare, the shipping company being unaware of his presence on board).

The freighter did not stop for long at any port, so, until his arrival at Cape Town, Panos remained unaware of how alien and estranging the world of foreigners could be. The natural pace of the island's inhabitants and the almost forced leisureliness of the holidaymakers who came to Mykonos had done little to prepare him for the frantic bustle of a big city at rush hour.

Most baffling to Panos were the numerous Africans dressed in European clothing who hurried down the streets laughing, chattering, and shouldering one another and him out of the way. Panos had seen black men working at the docks of other African ports, but he had somehow imagined them living in a state of savage grace far from the kind of city that *he* would inhabit. Yet here they were: talking an English too fast for him to understand more than the occasional word, dressed not in leopard skins and beads but in clothes like his own. Panos felt lost and somehow disappointed, and when a tall and wild-eyed African begged him for "Sixpence please, baas," he nervously handed the man whatever small change he could find in his pocket.

It was only after Panos had been in the country a few days and had spent numerous hours on the train to Johannesburg that he began to feel less uneasy about Africans. Their strange vitality with its undertones of violence and destruction that had so unnerved him on his arrival, now seemed contained and barely notice-able. The Africans that he saw from the safety of the train were either potbellied children who begged for pennies or sweets; large, swaybacked, odoriferous women who aggressively tried to sell him beaded neck-laces, carved animals, or sugarcane at the various train stops; or gaunt and lonely cowherds driving their scrofular cattle over the grassless, dusty hillsides. The train moved with a slow and steady beat and helped to take away the sensation of speeded-up time that had first assailed him on his arrival. Now he began to feel a sense of desolation, of contempt for the arid land and its peoples. Looking out of the train window, Panos kept remembering how the ship steward described the country as "forgotten by God." He was unmoved by even the beauty of the looming dragon-winged moun-tains, or the charms of the bare-breasted, ocher-daubed Xhosa women. It was June—midwinter, the droughty season—and Panos saw only the land, barren and end-less.

Johannesburg was frenzied on a far greater scale than Cape Town, but Panos was better able to deal with it—if only thanks to the druglike somnolence induced in him by the long train ride. He managed to find a taxi after some timid hailing on a corner outside the train station. The taxi driver shook his head at the address, which Panos had painstakingly copied onto the back of a railroad timetable. Finally, after Panos agreed to pay the return fare as well, the taxi driver (who was himself an immigrant) relented. Panos was to regret the man's acquiescence, for their destination proved to be an hour's drive away, at the very outskirts of the city, and the ride cost him a sizable chunk of his dwindling cash supply. Given the confusing size and extent of the city, he did realize, however, that it would have been fruitless for him to have tried to find the place himself.

The shop was open, its lights on, and Panos walked in to be met by a middle-aged Greek woman whom he took to be his uncle's wife. The woman informed him that Konstantin Kristianos had died of tuberculosis some two weeks before. Panos also learned that she was not in fact his uncle's wife, but the wife of the Greek owner of a liquor store a few streets down.

"If you leave a shop closed around here, even for just a few days, thieves will break in and steal everything."

She did not ask payment for the two weeks that she had taken care of the grocery store, nor did Panos offer any. It was an unstated but understood fact that he would have a difficult enough time paying his uncle's funeral expenses and keeping the shop open. The shop itself was shabby and smelled of must, and the district that it served was far from the center of the city and poor. Panos knew little of the workings of groceries, but it was obvious to him that the bulk of the old man's savings had been in what he sent to Greece, that the dead man had never been prosperous. Panos's frustration did not allow him to show gratitude to the bottle-store owner and his wife. On the contrary, it bothered him that he was in a position of debt to them and he answered their invitations to drop by with a curt: "I'm sorry. I have no time." Whenever one of them came into his store, it reminded him of the sorry position he now found himself in and he could not help being unfriendly and taciturn. After a while the visits stopped; although, on seeing Panos in the street, the old bottle-store owner would raise a casual hand in greeting.

At first, Panos used what was left of the money he had been sent to make innovations in the shop. He cleaned off and added to the dusty tins of Greek delicacies which he found in a storage room in the rear, and he built an extra shelf in the store window to give them "more prominent display" (a phrase he acquired from a box containing long-unsold chocolate Easter eggs). He also hired an electrician—for what he later realized was an inordinately large sum—to put up a neon sign outside the grocery. The sign read: PANOS'S GROCERY SHOPPE. The last two letters were an artistic touch, "done for nothing," as Panos proudly told some of his early customers. Each letter was a foot high, and Panos imagined the sign lighting up the night sky, a beacon for shoppers from miles away.

"All you have to do now is sit back and let the customers roll in," the electrician remarked, carefully folding the pound notes he had received in payment and slipping them into the front pocket of his grease-stained work shirt.

The sign attracted a fair-sized crowd of Africans at its construction, who expressed their admiration with much enthusiasm but did not come into the store. Panos's clients proved to be mainly poor whites and Africans, who would probably have been just as likely to come to the store to buy their few staples had there been no sign outside at all. Panos tried to speak to them in his adept though ungrammatical English, but the Africans merely shifted from one foot to another and looked away in embarrassment ... while the whites would choose the occasion to beg for credit. Panos soon

realized that he had little in common with his customers and gave up these ill-fated attempts at conversation. He would gaze dejectedly at the old wooden sign
reposing amidst the rubbish in the empty lot at the
back of the shop, and he would worry about the decline
in his precious funds. The only things that he sold were
the low-profit daily items: milk, bread, *mielie-meal*
(for the African's staple porridge), the occasional
newspaper, and the narrow sticks of sun-dried meat
known as *biltong*. The tarama roe, the calamata olives,
the Genuine Extra-Virgin Olive Oil in half- and one-
gallon cans, once more began to gather dust and were
gradually replaced by loaves of cheap white bread and
family-size bottles of Coca-Cola. And then the electric
sign that he had been so proud of began to bear witness
to its shoddy construction. After only three or four
months, almost a quarter of the letters had ceased to
function. The sign had come to read: PA OS'S GRO ER
SHO .

Panos had never been a particularly energetic man
and the failure of his first attempts at creative redecor-
ation made him take a desultory, almost indifferent
approach to further improvements. Still, his lingering
desire to make the shop profitable made him easy prey
for the occasional unscrupulous retail man who talked
him into buying a number of items he did not need and
could not possibly sell—cigars that had rapidly gone
stale in their tobacco-reeking wooden cabinets; key
rings in the shape of maps of South African provinces
or of animals; and other novelties that might have sold
well in a resort area, but which languished unbought
on the counter until they were obscured by newspapers,
boxes of candy, and cartons of cigarettes. Perhaps the
only new purchase of any value was a tall coffee machine that came to occupy pride of place on a shelf to
the right of Panos's chair behind the counter. The

money made from the infrequent cups of coffee that he sold was not enough to justify the initial outlay for the machine, but at least it was not a total loss and Panos now had a ready supply of steaming mugs of strong hot coffee. This was to be his final and most successful innovative buy. The early salesmen had been able to get around Panos's peasant shrewdness by praising his business acumen in recognizing the clear superiority of their particular product. As his capital decreased and Panos realized the uselessness of arguing with salesmen, he hit upon the recourse of meeting all but their initial inquiries with a stony, unreceptive silence. This proved enough to turn away even the most persistent traveling retailers. Nevertheless, Panos wrote to his family that things were going well and that he was in touch with the big Johannesburg merchants.

Shortly after his arrival, when he was still curious about the new country, Panos would leave the shop closed on Sundays and take a bus into the city. At first he visited the popular and populated shopping districts—Hillbrow, the Killarney Centre, or Rosebank. He enjoyed looking at the well-to-do people and walking around the expensive shops that did not even allow Africans inside, let alone have to rely on them for business. Panos liked to imagine himself owning one of these stores and he always felt affronted if a store assistant asked him if he needed help. He would stand in front of the better shops and consider what their names would be were they his own. Thus, Barney's Haberdashery became the Demitopoulos Haberdashery, Christie's Delicatessen became Panos's Greek Food Store, and the English Cottage became the Mykonos Inn. It was a pleasant way to spend an afternoon, but it started to become tedious as time went on, a reminder that there had been no change in Panos's

everyday fortunes. He also noticed that he had begun
to attract curious glances from the shopkeepers and
passersby as he stood bemused before a storefront window. One day, attracted by the name, he boarded a bus
marked Herman Eckstein Park and shortly found himself at the Johannesburg Zoo. It gave him a disquieting
pleasure to examine the strange animals, many of
whose cages bore the legend: ''These animals formerly
roamed wild in the very area their cages are now.''
Watching the huge and gentle eland being fed peanuts
by groups of schoolchildren who perched on the guard
railings, or being himself coldly observed by a motion-
less S-shaped green mamba poised on a branch in the
snake pit, Panos marveled at the thin barriers that
separated this country's present from its savage past.

Panos continued to visit the zoo and zoo lake area
for several more months, ruminating often on the
thought that the land's present placidity was merely
an accident of time. He felt most at ease under the
shade of a large weeping willow, from where he would
regard the amorous young couples boating on the lake
or occasionally be surprised by a colorful procession of
Indian wedding-goers. He avoided the plot set aside
for artists to exhibit their work—where crowds of people tended to gather—as well as the east side of the
lake, where a small flock of ducks in search of crusts of
bread raucously accosted passersby. Instead, he rested
becalmed underneath his tree, for hours on end watching ripples break across the bows of the rowboats, his
mind content with the play of light on the surface of
the water. But summer was fast approaching. The days
were growing hotter with each passing week; the animal cages began to give off a pungent odor of baked
dung, the inhabitants huddling together in the dimness
of their narrow hutches; the sun's reflection off the
lake penetrated the very depths of the willow's shade,

making Panos's eyes ache; and the bus rides home were stifling, seeming longer every time. With each excursion into the sun-drenched outdoors, Panos found himself craving more strongly the comforting gloom of the grocery. After a time he became increasingly reluctant to leave the store at all, putting off his outing to the following week and then the week after that.

It was summer and the cool interior of the grocery was infinitely more appealing than the before-the-storm, blinding, sweltering dazzle of the world outside. Panos idly read paragraphs of the Sunday newspaper, dwelling on the accounts of accidents and assaults. The coffee machine was bubbling pleasantly beside him; his large white mug was full with the brown, strong-smelling liquid. In his mouth were two hard candies of different flavor. Panos slowly turned the sweets around and around with his tongue while he read, savoring the contrast in tastes. Every now and then, he would take a large mouthful of coffee, hold it puffed between his cheeks for a moment, and then swallow it, feeling the gradual return of the candy's flavor. His chair had been moved closer to the window and the extra shelf (which had obstructed his vision of the street) had been removed. He could read, observe the pavement outside, enjoy his sweets and coffee, and even serve his customers without hardly moving from his seat. He had grown heavier, and the tan acquired from his long-past Sunday jaunts had gone sallow.

Panos looked up with surprise as a shiny and expensive-looking car, driven by a smart-capped black chauffeur, pulled up in front of the grocery. A well-dressed man climbed out of the back, marched into the grocery, and bought two Sunday papers from the resolutely sullen and torpid Panos. The grocer watched the smoothly receding rear of the car with some amazement. Wealthy people in chauffeur-driven cars were rarely seen in his district, and the knowledge was heavy in him that the rich man was merely passing through. Panos threw his newspaper away from him in a sudden burst of fury. He, Panos Demitopoulos, was not going to sit there as inactive as the sacks of mielie-meal on his shelves. He would do something energetic. He would find a way to make himself rich! Then we would see who drove a nice car.

To help him think, Panos decided to walk until an idea came to him. He locked up the shop and walked away from it, in the opposite direction of the city. He strode swiftly, and now and then he smiled deliberately to himself. He did not have any ideas just yet, but they would come. A playful wind tossed bits of debris and dust in the air around him, stinging his eyes, but this did not bother him as it ordinarily would have. He marched forward, looking straight in front of him, trying to convey a sense of purposefulness in the tilt of his head, the speed of his stride, and the force of his gaze. He took little notice of the decrepit houses to either side of him, the dusty and litter-filled street, the thin dogs that flitted in and out of the alleyways or busied themselves with the rubbish bins. All he could see were the golden mine dumps shining in the distance and, beyond them, the outcropping ridges of the Magaliesberg glinting in the afternoon sun. Panos stopped, and looked with pleased if somewhat forced interest at the width and spaciousness of the horizon before him. To dramatize the effect, he turned and looked toward where he had just come from, toward the city itself. The dark cloud moving unhurriedly from behind and around the distant city made the view resemble a gigantic, narrowing funnel.

Panos realized how hot it was, how hot *he* was. The wind had died down, and all that was left was an overriding oppressiveness. As he was taking off his light summer jacket in an effort to cool down, he noticed that several dogs had followed him and appeared to be waiting for his next move. They were rangy and vicious-looking and Panos wondered whether he ought not to throw a stone at them. A drop of sweat ran down his forehead and trickled down the side of his nose. It was better to ignore them and walk away. He put his jacket on with a convulsive movement and started walking quickly toward the mines, toward the mountains. The dogs did not bark, but he could hear their low growling and the intermittent snarl. He could sense them moving behind him. If only they would bark! Panos turned around again, noticing that the number of dogs had grown. He was about to turn and run from the bristling, hostile pack when a large, dirty white mastiff rushed suddenly forward and seized him by the thigh, then stood holding him, a fierce snarl rumbling throughout its body. Panos tried to force the beast's jaws open, but it growled menacingly and bit down harder. He was afraid to do anything more, lest the other dogs come to the aid of their leader, but he could not just stand there perspiring while the pain in his leg got worse!

"Hey. *Voetsek, blerry hond. Laas hom, laas hom nou.*" An African woman was coming forward from one of the dirty shacks nearby. She was shouting and beating a large iron pot with a wooden spoon. The pack of dogs fled. The mastiff, seeing that it had been deserted, released its hold and walked stiffly away.

"Baas, you okay?" The woman regarded him with mingled pity and amusement. Panos looked up from gently feeling the bite on his leg and nodded. "Baas, if the dogs start following you, just pretend to pick up a stone. They'll *skrik* and run off."

Panos muttered his thanks and began to limp back toward the grocery.

"Here, baas, let me put some water on that leg. It must be sore."

Panos glanced down at the torn patch of trouser high on his upper leg, shook his head, and walked away. Slowly, with his head down, he limped along the way back to his store, ignoring the stares and unspoken questions of the few people he passed. When he had almost reached the grocery, he passed a group of Africans who were chatting together as they leaned against a partially demolished wall. One of them caught a glimpse of his bloody trouser leg and grim expression, and yelled with laughter: "Heh! It must have been the baasie's first time!"

The other Africans also laughed and shouted ribaldries in their own tongue. Panos scowled even more angrily and walked on. The African who had made the joke called after him, "You all right, boss?" But Panos pretended that he had heard neither the remark nor the evidently solicitous question.

Panos reached the grocery as the first drops of rain began to fall. He went inside, bathed his wound and painted it with iodine, wrapped a piece of clean but torn sheet around his leg, and changed into another pair of trousers. He then turned on the lights in the store and plugged in the neon sign outside, put some fresh water in the coffee machine, and emptied and scrubbed out his coffee mug. By this time, the rain was falling harder, the sky had become dark, and thunder could be heard. The raindrops struck the glass pane, settled for a moment, and then began the slow journey of sliding down the glass, speeding up only when they met and engulfed one of their fellows.

C A R I L L O N

I am standing at 42nd and Lexington, the busiest corner in New York...if not the world. It is my lunch
hour and I have just finished eating my tunafish sandwich in the lobby of the Philip Morris Building and
have come here to watch the people go by: 40,000 of
them pass this spot every hour, I once read. My great-
grandfather spent his entire lifetime in a small Welsh
town whose population, when I visited a year ago, was
eight hundred and sixteen. So, in the past fifteen minutes I have certainly seen more people than he saw in
his span of seventy years. The crowd flows by me in its
multitude—solid, immutable, and infinitely varied,
filled with purpose.

Recently I have found myself thinking about an incident that took place on the Hamburg *Schnellzug*.
An exhausted Turk or Iranian—one of those whom

my friend Chris wickedly referred to as "Gassed-workers"—sat slumped on a seat near me with a large duffel bag at his feet. A well-dressed and imposing German businessman got on board and began to berate him for blocking the aisle. When the Turk wearily protested, the businessman gave the bag a contemptuous push with one elegantly shod foot, drew himself to his full height and intoned: *"Sie wissen ja gar nicht wer ich bin!"* (Clearly, you have no idea who I am!) I longed to ask him who he was but in this, as in so many things, I lacked the courage until it was too late. But his comment has become my theme song and I murmur it to myself whenever my spirits flag.

These figures pass by me. Their elbows are far too solid for them to be wraiths, but they are alien and their eyes glitter hard and unknowable. I do not exist for them. I long to cry out, *"Sie wissen ja gar nicht wer ich bin!"* but time is wearing on and I too join the streaming horde. Beside me, the high heels of two secretaries mockingly tap out the question: *"Wer bin ich? Wer bin ich?"* I catch a glimpse of myself in a storefront window and wonder: Who is this girl, her head cocked to one side, lost in thought in the elegant anonymity of Midtown? Silly, small, alone.

I picture the little "thinking" vein on my lover's temple, the autonomous life of his long-fingered hands. If Mark were here, he could hold me, shield off the frightening parody of these *others* who breathe and walk and chatter in such alarming numbers. It is often like this. At intervals during the day I will have a sudden, absolutely physical need to have him near me. Yet I know that when I get home, drained from the day's work, I will want only to read in the kitchen undisturbed by his attentions. That I will be angry with him for intruding on my solitude and for thinking that he can do so because it is *his* apartment. That I will be mean and hateful and cruel to him. That I cannot help myself.

I walk swiftly now, since I have gone at least twenty minutes over my lunch hour (or half-hour, as it should be known). I enter the Hamilton Building and am soon seated at my desk, where the gray screen of my computer terminal waits for me to breathe amber life into it. I am working as a temporary this summer, inputting figures for the database of a large insurance company. I detest my job. I simply don't understand how people can live this way: their minds disengaged, their bodies in the semblance of motion. I would kill myself before I accepted that this is how I should always pass my days.

No one seems to have noticed my prolonged absence, so I am doubly glad that I snatched those extra minutes of freedom. I let my fingers fly across the keys, making a game of how fast I can transfer information from paper to the screen. Columns of figures form and blur in front of my eyes.

"Whoa. You're making me dizzy," a voice behind me calls.

Bill Remick has come by to drop off some more columns for me to input. He sits on top of my desk, breathing a coffee smell. I'm happy to see him and ask him what's new.

Bill tells me that the other office workers wonder about me, they think me strange. He is always saying what a great time he has with the other temps, yet I never seem to find anything to talk to them about. It is strange that Bill with his high, whiny voice and sallow features has become part of the "in" crowd at Republican Insurance. I was the first person to befriend him, but lately I get the feeling he thinks I should feel privileged that he still associates with me.

"I defended you," Bill says smugly. He waves his

foot as he balances on my desk. His pants leg is too short and I stare in disgust at the white expanse of pudgy calf between it and the top of his sock.

"So, do you want to go to a movie tonight?" he asks.

Once he leaves, I punch furiously at the keyboard without paying attention to what I am doing. Gossip, gossip, gossip. It was the same at school, where people I did not know well enough to say hello to knew (or thought they knew) about my every move. In small, self-contained institutions people become like laboratory mice that nibble at each other, create little dramas, assign one flat adjective per character. I often think I would be best off living alone in a houseboat, emerging only to buy supplies from one trusted grocery run by a deaf-mute.

I soon finish all the papers on my desk, but I know better than to go and ask for more work. One reason the other temporaries don't like me is that I get things done too quickly while they seek only to do the bare minimum. Even my supervisor, Bob Smyth, was getting upset with my constant requests for something else to do, as though appalled by my seemingly insatiable appetite for work. He's about thirty and has a round, vacant but pleasant face. He came by my desk shortly after he'd told me to slow down, and found me reading a book. "Don't do that," he said. "Look busy, or you make me look bad." None of this makes any sense.

I create a new file and amuse myself for a while by typing in as much of "The Dong with the Luminous Nose" as I can remember. Perhaps some future accountant will call up the file, Nose. Perhaps he or she will have a revelation after reading it and abandon insurance to join the circus.

I have forgotten the last verse of the Lear poem, and now I type in: _M_adly _a_morous _r_omantic _k_itten; _M_y

African rambunctious kaleidoscope; Must adults remain koans? Mark started this game. We were sitting outside of Café Reggio in the Village when he grabbed a napkin and began writing. Kangaroos yawn lovingly in excitement. As he spelled out my name, each word seemed to caress me. Kissing your lovely Irish eyes; Kinglike, you lustfully incite embraces. What a hopeless romantic he is. At times it makes me melt with pleasure; at other times, I am repelled.

I met Mark under impossibly romantic circumstances. I was eighteen and it was a few weeks before I left my hometown in Southern California forever and before I spent that first year in Germany. I grew up in Solana Beach, the kind of place that made Germans exclaim: *"Ach, sie kommen von einem Paradis."* If you were born beautiful and you believed that God ordained that you should only experience physical pleasure *and* you believed that nothing else existed in the world, then this was indeed your paradise. For me, it was hell with palm trees. I envied my school friends for being so happy and hated them for being so vacuous. They, in turn, categorized me as "a brain" and ignored me except for when they were faced with a particularly difficult homework problem. I went to what was supposed to be a good school and it probably was, though how could anyone be expected to have any worthwhile thoughts or profound emotions in a place so airy and light? Why, when our poetry teacher wanted to stir up the muse in all of us, she passed around several freshly plucked roses from her garden and asked us to look at, touch, sniff, and comment upon them. A surfer behind me said: "It's just a fucking rose."

Of course, there were things I liked about California ... although they were not necessarily things I could share with many people. Baking in the hot sun on the beach all day did nothing for me, but the way my dog smelled after we hiked through the sagebrush in the canyons was pure ecstasy. And, in winter, heavy fog would sometimes blanket the beach, turning passersby into soft, veiled figures that loomed and then disappeared. There was a spot you could go to at low tide where sand, sea, and sky all met to become the same diffuse gray. I would stand there for hours, at peace in a world without boundaries.

I met Mark at a beach party that Ron, the pedantic graduate student I was "seeing," took me to. I rarely went to parties and I wasn't enjoying this one. I sat at the edge of the firelit crowd watching the others as they chattered away and roasted hot dogs on the ends of coat hangers. I was wondering how I could persuade Ron to drive me home when this slim, blond fellow came up and sat beside me. I had noticed him before, taken him to be just another UCSD grad student—that oxymoron, the surfer-intellectual—and was surprised that he paid any attention to me. But his face was kind and ascetic behind the spectacles that reflected twin campfires, and his voice was . . . well, the best word would be old. Mature, toned-down, wise, with the faintest tinge of an accent. It was a pleasant voice to listen to as he told me how much he loved California after sundown, when the scent of Cleveland sage filled the air and the night was suffused with the sighing of waves as they slipped down the beach.

He asked if I wanted to take a walk, and so we abandoned the noise and drunkenness of the circle of fire and strolled south along the littoral, letting the ocean foam wet our bare feet. We walked for miles, all the way to Torrey Pines, stopping occasionally to watch the ocean. The water was unusually warm that year and it flickered with phosphorescent copepods, tiny shrimp that lit the paths of leaping fish. At one point

Mark asked me if I wanted to swim, but I said no, I was afraid of the ocean and especially at night.

"I know this spot. It's quite safe," he persisted.

"No, I don't want to."

He disappeared into the shadows of the cliffs for a moment and then his gleaming body flashed by me and he was in the ocean, a greenish glimmer marking his trail through the water. I used to love swimming in the sea until one day, while floating on my back, I felt myself being absorbed into its vast movement. I lost my sense of direction and began to thrash around wildly, and although I made it back to shore without help, I have never since been able to swim without thinking of the ocean's awesome force, the hugeness of its tides, the myriad disgusting creatures that lurk in its depths.

Mark soon returned, shaking the water out of his curly hair like a dog. He had kept on his underwear, which clung to him, and I noticed that he was lean and well muscled. He got dressed, gave me a light, chilled kiss on the cheek, and we resumed walking.

It's funny how I haven't lost a single detail of that night. Not Mark's stories of his childhood in South Africa and his descriptions of the odd series of jobs he'd held in the past few years: maintenance worker in a high rise, bookstore clerk, "counter person" in a coffee shop ("I felt like some kind of anti-matter"), teacher in a private high school. Nor how I quickly wrote my telephone number on a page pulled out of my pocket diary and, feeling terribly bold and shameless, slipped it into his pocket as we said goodnight.

I thought of Mark often that year in Germany. He had been strangely shy of making love with someone barely a year older than his students, but his lovemaking was gentle and attentive—how different from the brutishness of the bartender who claimed my virginity

in his tatterdemalion beach house (''Jeez, I didn't
know it was your first time'') and from Ron's needy
self-absorption. I thought of him often, but his letters
were desultory and far between and the parade of men
on my ''European tour'' served to ease him from my
memory.

We remet a year and a half ago when I was visiting
my mother in California at Christmas and he called
on the off-chance that I would be there. We stayed
friends, wrote the occasional amiable noncommittal letter. Then he moved to Weehawken just across the river
from Manhattan and I stopped by to visit for a few
days this past spring break. I was planning to sleep on
the couch, but something in the way his eyes smiled at
me as we sat drinking beer at the Monkey Bar made
me change my mind.

Someone announces that the coffee wagon has arrived. I abandon my computer and reverie and go buy
myself a cup of tea, glad that the afternoon is approaching its end. I try to resist the sight of the dis-
gustingly yummy junk food that hangs in plastic bags
from hooks on the wagon and I escape into the mail
room where Bill is sitting with Kate and Marianne, two
fellow temps. Bill munches a pink Hostess cupcake and
blows noisily on his coffee to cool it down.

''We were just talking about how Kate is getting
over the hill,'' he says.

Kate comes over to me and holds out a strand of
silverish hair.

''I'm thirty,'' she says. ''I'm still in school, and I've
got *gray* hair!''

''Seriously,'' she continues. ''It's terrible getting
old. Nobody wants you anymore. Your boobs start to
sag. Even Bill's.''

I like Kate, who is a part-time graduate student in

history and has stylishly cropped hair, a pixie-ish face and a dancer's compact body. She's not always friendly, but she has a wonderful straightforward manner and I often wish I could be like her. I detest Marianne, however, though I had a huge crush on her when I first met her. She has this lovely Modigliani face and an assured walk. I watched admiringly from a distance until I discovered that she writes in a childishly large scrawl and is given to saying things like: "That was *sooo* fun." I give her a long, cold stare until she flounces out of the room in a snit.

These crushes overwhelm me: I will find someone impossibly beautiful, distant, intriguing. Men and women. The crushes don't last and are often wasted on someone totally unworthy, but I wouldn't give them up for all the world. It's like biting into a cold peach; I get goosebumps all over. Mark is different and he doesn't understand my infatuations. His affection is constant and unchanging: a wide and placid river emptying endlessly into the sea. I couldn't possibly be like that. When I have one of my crushes, I want to be that person, crawl inside his skin, feel his blood pulse through my veins.

For me, love is all-important and redemptive. It has replaced religion and God. It doesn't matter that it blazes only for an instant before vanishing without trace. It doesn't matter that I often despair of ever being able to love anyone in a true, sustained way. It's the believing in its existence that counts.

This is not a popular view these days. Most of the people I know want to give the impression of being unimpassioned about their love affairs. At a recent party given by my friend Mary and her boyfriend, Peter, I watched as she grabbed the hand of a former lover of hers and led him into a bedroom. I was talking to Peter at the time, and I knew by the look of baffled pain on his handsome face that he, too, had seen. They were gone for a long time, but Peter continued talking to me in a cheerful, nonchalant voice, his eyes occasionally flickering over to the closed door behind me.

"I really didn't like what you did," I told Mary when we got together a few days later. I realized only then how angry this incident had made me, and I tried to pinpoint what it was that bothered me. "I hate to see someone gratuitously hurt."

"All Jim and I did was talk," Mary said in surprise. "Well, kiss a little. But Peter didn't mind. We don't believe in jealousy and all that stuff."

We were walking a few paces behind Peter and another friend, and Mary hurried to catch up. "You weren't mad that I went off to be alone with Jim?" she asked.

"No, of course not." His reply was immediate and there was nothing in his glance to suggest he felt otherwise.

Five o'clock. The chutes open and the office workers drain out the first floor of the building. Bill Remick walks me through Madison Square Park and up Broadway. I notice that he has a boil on his neck which he fingers speculatively. "You sure you don't want to take in a movie?"

"Yes. I want to finish my book."

Unbidden, he reaches into the side of my bag and takes out *Orlando*. "Jesus, Kylie, you're such a cliché. Nobody reads Virginia Woolf any more."

We part at Broadway and I continue walking uptown, annoyed at his persistence but already beginning to feel lonely and to wish I had gone with him. Mark teaches at the community college tonight and will not be home until late, and, while I have been looking forward to solitude all week long, now that the moment has arrived I find myself afraid of it.

At the next traffic light, I notice a pregnant black

woman with beautiful, mobile features talking to another woman.

"I don't go to funerals when I'm pregnant," she says. "I don't believe in that. Birth. Death. To carry life and see something like that. Nuh-uh."

I watch her in fascination. She seems radiant, so sure of herself and of the life she is carrying. I wonder if I will ever have the courage to do what she is doing. I walk on, bemused, but am jolted into awareness by the blast of a truck horn at the next corner. I look up, trembling from the sudden noise, to see a brawny man in a muscle shirt leering at me and making pointed gestures at my breasts. I quickly cross the street, followed by his inane laughter.

It is always this way in the city; one is constantly defiled, touched by the vile imaginings and indiscriminate desires of men. Kate told me that she had gotten so angry at a man on the sidewalk who kept blocking her way ("one of those middle-aged Spanish guys in a sweaty undershirt, with a stomach like he'd swallowed a basketball") that she spat in his face. I could never do something like that, though after each such encounter I am consumed with rage.

I walk west on 42nd Street, past the sex films featuring "real live virgins" and past the sleazy men in shop foyers who whisper, "Hey, baby, come here. I've got something to show you." Hot smoke blows in my face and my nostrils are assaulted by the acrid smell of charred meat as I pass the kebab vendors' stands. Once I bought one of their sandwiches on my way to meet a friend and stopped in the park to eat it. The meat had not been properly cooked, and when I opened the tinfoil wrapper the pale bread lay raw and bloody inside like a gutted fish, while blood dripped on my hands, legs, dress.

At last I reach the Port Authority and climb into

one of the Cuban mini-vans that shuttle back and forth
between Weehawken and Manhattan. I find myself
firmly wedged between a young woman wearing pan-
cake makeup and an older man in a lightweight poly-
ester suit. The van is stuffy and hot and all the seats
are filled, but the driver seems in no hurry to leave.
Some of the passengers chatter cheerfully to one another; the woman next to me takes out a copy of *Self*
magazine and begins to fill out a questionnaire about
her sex life; the businessman twists and turns in his
seat, his leg uncomfortably warm against mine. I close
my eyes and try to shut out this world for a while.

I hate this commute and wish I could afford to live
almost anywhere other than where I am living. I had
not intended to live with Mark this summer, and, in
fact, our enforced proximity has already almost destroyed our relationship. I had wanted to see him, to be
with him, to make love to him . . . but living with him
made it seem as if these things were required, as if I
were paying rent with my body.

Initially, my friend and former study partner from
school, Nelson, had invited me to stay with him in the
Village, where he was house-sitting while his parents
were away. I had stayed with him before and we had
gotten along well, enjoyed each other as friends, re-
spected one another's boundaries, so I hadn't given it
another thought, especially as I knew it was a large
apartment.

We had a pleasant dinner at a nearby Middle East-
ern restaurant the night I arrived, although I was tired
from the long bus journey from the language school in
Vermont and Nelson complained too frequently about
not having been able to find a girlfriend this summer.
When we returned to his apartment, I pulled off my
shoes and settled down on the couch to read. Nelson
said something lame about how I must be tired and

then sat down beside me and began to paw at me. I pushed him roughly away. There had never been anything between us, and I just wanted to be left alone.

Nelson stalked around the room, moving objects about. His jaw clenched tight, he banged down a book here, replaced a glass there.

"I don't know what's the matter with you," he muttered.

"There's nothing wrong with me," I exploded. "You're the one who's got a problem."

It was as if someone had flicked a switch and in an instant we were shouting accusations at each other. Nelson claimed that I was just using him. I complained that he was abusing our friendship.

"You usually don't care who you sleep with," he said at last, bitterly.

I regretted telling Nelson about my experiments with sleeping around in Germany and was instantly mad with anger that he should throw it up at me this way. Why couldn't he understand? My friend Chris in Berlin had understood, and he had his own word for me: he called me a nympholeptic, one who is "seized by nymphs," who is always seeking the unattainable. Strange, sardonic Christophe. I slept with him the first night I met him and in the morning he said, "Good, now that we've got that over with we can be friends." Although he mocked at me and could be bitingly critical, Chris knew me in a way no one else ever has. At least he understood why I would grab at those moments of ecstasy, even knowing they are only match flares in the dark.

I almost miss my stop and have to yell at the driver to let me out at the traffic light. There is no mail for me and the vestibule is depressingly ill lit, the climb to the fourth floor redolent of moldy wallpaper. The hall light is on inside the apartment. It is always on. Mark is renting the place temporarily from someone he met at one of his free-lance jobs, and one condition of the rental is that this light must never be turned off.

"When I was a kid, my father was always saying 'Shut the light, shut the light,' " the apartment owner, Jack Karowski, told Mark. His father was now in an old-age home and Jack was convinced that the only thing keeping him alive was this light bulb he burned in his honor. His cousin occasionally looked in on the place, and unbeknownst to Jack, replaced the light at regular intervals.

"He's a strange fellow," Mark told me. "I had to take down endless amounts of junk from the walls when I first moved in here."

In the storage closet are hand-painted five-pointed stars to meditate on, books about self-visualization and -actualization, Baba Ram Das's *BE HERE NOW!!*, and plastic stick-on rainbows that Mark had carefully unpeeled from the windowpanes.

I am here now and I think of turning out the light just to see what will happen, but I decide against severing the thin thread that holds poor Mr. Karowski still dangling in this vale of tears. Instead, I make myself some spaghetti and a salad, which I eat while watching the sunset reflected in the myriad windows of Manhattan. It's a large, light apartment with a spectacular view of the river and the city, although this often serves simply to remind one that life is going on over there, not here. I watch the progress of a police car's flashing lights going up the crowded West Side Highway until they disappear from view. Looking down to my right about two hundred yards, I can just make out the park where Alexander Hamilton was shot, sinking onto the green grass now fouled by dogs, the city and its promises so close he could have reached a hand out and touched it.

I would like to write a poem but I cannot think what it would be about. I can picture myself sitting here, carefully shaping out the lines and phrases. I rinse my dishes and sit down again at the oak kitchen table with my fountain pen uncapped and paper in front of me, but the words I'm seeking are not there. I'm too restless to think. I light a cigarette. My throat is sore from smoking too much, yet I hope the cigarette will let me bear down on my life. It's the wonderful thing about smoking; it gives you a focal point, if only for a moment. "Find me a fixed point," Einstein said, "and I will move the universe."

Still nothing. I pour myself a glass of coarse red wine, take my book, and lie on the couch in front of the bay window. But the words on the page seem to crowd together to hide their meaning from me. I lay down the book, put a tape on, and light myself a cigarette. The Andean flutes of Inti-Illimani fill the room as I watch the lights of tugboats drifting down the Hudson. Mark has told me that the most gaily lit boats are the wide, flat garbage scows, but from here they all appear to be enchanted ships embarking on a magical journey. I sip the wine. It is harsh, burrs my tongue, warms my lips. The blue smoke of my cigarette curls toward the ceiling, and I amuse myself by blowing smoke rings that curl and eddy in some unseen draft. A boat chugs up the river to the throaty passionate voices and the intake of breath on the flutes. A string of jewels marks its rigging.

The moment contrives itself into perfection. I feel the hand of the deity gently rocking the earth. There are several gods in my pantheon : the harsh one who demands I search ever forward; the glassblower who creates these crystallized moments of perfection; the goat god who makes love to me in the woods, his instruments the wind and the scent of flowers, the loamy smell of earth.

I want to writhe in pure sensuality like a cat. That soft lamp glow on the armchair reminds me of Mark's cheek in the morning, stubbled with light blond hairs. Such contrast, the soft skin hot to the touch, the harsh sandpaper of his beard, the hard unyielding cheekbone, the baby-fine hair.

There is a fumbling of keys at the lock. The door creaks open, bangs shut, and there is a sigh of animal relief at being home. And how can I think of him with voluptuous tenderness when he is moving obtrusively around the room, banging books down on the table, smiling at me in friendly greeting, understanding nothing?

Mark starts to tell me cheerfully about his day. "We've been reading *Diary of a Madman*," he says. "It was a typical class, everyone sitting dumbly waiting for me to tell them what the story means. Then that Chinese student, Sing, the one who hasn't said a word all semester, spoke up. 'It's about my life,' he said. That's all. 'It's about my life.' "

Mark likes to tell stories. Everything becomes an anecdote with him, and somehow, when we walk along the street we see "incidents," things that could become a story. I like the way he tells these tales, but I never know what they mean, if anything. He could be telling them to anyone, with the same cheerful detached voice. There is this inaccessible core to him—another person watching the world from behind his eyes. I find myself growing hugely irritated as he tells me one fascinating incident after another, none of which bring me any closer to that underground stream that I imagine to be there, silent, deep and swift.

We talk for a while and then I retire to my room where, by means of undoing various hooks and moving cushions about, I turn the couch/ottoman into a bed. I told Mark about a week ago that I wanted to move out, that it was too much like a transaction to be his lover

and live off him. To my surprise, he suggested I move
into the other room. I was in dread of a repeat of the
scene with Nelson and had even made some desultory
inquiries into women's hostels, but Mark is the perfect
gentleman, the niceness not just a facade.

After a time he comes in to say goodnight. We hug
and caress until he says, "I guess it's time for me to
go?" The door closes softly behind him and I am left
missing his strong, encircling arm and thinking he
should really know when it's time to stop being a
gentleman. I wonder if I'm just being a tease, but that
seems too blunt and simple a word for what is all so
complicated.

I am up early in the morning, my favorite time of
day. I drink rich black coffee, eat buttered toast with
apricot preserves, and contemplate the silky morning
light. A shaft of sunlight illuminates the kitchen table,
though clouds scud over the city and it is freakishly
autumn cool for a day in late August. I go into Mark's
room and watch him sleep. He mumbles something and
moves his jaw up and down as if he is eating. I raise
one of the venetian-blind slats to take a look at the
newly hatched pigeons in a nest on the filth-bespattered
window ledge on the opposite side of the airshaft. "Our
babies," Mark calls them. They are pink and they
squirm and have only just begun to sprout feathers,
but they are strangely adorable. Their real mother,
who is ugly in the way of all city pigeons, inclines her
head and casts a worried glance in my direction. The
babies struggle toward her, their mouths gaping. I am
fascinated and repelled by their fierce neediness, their
determined life. Instinct is supposed to take over when
you become a mother, but I can't see it, not for me. As
I leave the room, Mark stirs again and sleepily murmurs my name.

The breeze blowing through the open window is chill, so I take my Chaplin jacket with me when I leave the apartment. I found the jacket for a dollar in the bargain bins outside Canal Jeans. It's from the 1930s, and now that I've sewn the tear where the label was and had the jacket dry-cleaned, it looks very chic. I close the door slowly so the click of the latch will not wake Mark and in my rush I almost knock over the tiny old lady who is standing bemused, keys in hand, outside the door next to ours. She tentatively pushes the key against the lock but without success. I watch her impatiently as she hesitantly tries this several times, then I take the keys from her, open the door, and hand them back to her.

"I can't open my door anymore," she says in a tremulous voice. "I'm going to have to go to the loony bin."

"Nonsense," I say cheerily, practically pushing her inside. "You'll be fine."

I flounce down the stairs, filled with my own young life and with regret at the worthless succor that is all I can offer this eighty-six-year-old woman who lives alone and has no family.

I'm just in time for my bus and, as the tunnel traffic is light, I find myself in Manhattan in fifteen minutes and soon catch another bus up the West Side. It's only ten o'clock and I won't be meeting my friend Hartley until eleven, so I walk over to Endicott Books. At the traffic light, a poorly dressed man with a curly beard and intense blue eyes stares at me. I notice that he stands bowlegged from the weight of the sack slung over his shoulder. He catches my stare, glares at me and hisses, "I'll smash your face."

I should be inured by now to the yells, curses, insults, and ugly sights of this city that is part wasteland, part fairy tale. Yet I find myself shaken by the vehement hatred in the man's voice and, barely fifty yards later

by the sight of an attractive young woman stepping over the sprawled and unconscious body of a man who lies with his head in a pool of liquid on the pavement, a bottle clutched in one hand. The clear bright sunlight shines on me as I walk by him.

At Endicott, I breeze through the new books, look at the various literary magazines and wonder which ones I would send work to if I ever write something, spend a long time deciding whether or not to buy a new translation of Celan that I all along know I cannot afford. I buy it anyway. After I leave the bookstore I stroll aimlessly for a while until I notice an unusual sign on the side of a building. It is the head of an African antelope, a nyala, which I easily recognize because the same head was on the musty-smelling cloth print Mark gave me before I went to Germany and which now hangs on my wall at college. I go down the steps and ring the doorbell. A tall, lugubrious young man opens the door and ushers me into a room filled with animal skulls. "We're having a special on human skeletons," he says. "Mostly children. Would you like to make an offer?"

"Good grief, no!" I reply, convinced that he is making fun of me.

"Oh," he says. "I thought you were an artist. We get a lot of them coming here who want to buy skeletons. You can also rent with a small deposit. Heads and hands are very popular."

The glass-topped case near me is filled with tiny skulls and skeletons, including the delicate, necklace-like filigree of an entire snake skeleton. The bird and monkey skulls are tiny, intricate, perfect, like the finest Japanese carvings, and I can see why artists would want to study them. The assistant explains to me that the bones are cleaned off by being buried in earth with tiny beetles that eat away the minutest scrap of flesh.

He leads me into a back room where there are five or six skeletons and several enormous skulls of hippopotamus or elephant.

"You can tell something of the life that was led by the look of the bones," the assistant tells me, indicating one of the grinning relics. "This woman, for instance, was malnourished during her childhood."

" 'The evil that men do lives after them, the good is oft interred with their bones,' " I recite, pleased that I can remember the quote.

"Actually, the skeleton keeps a record of everything: the good and the bad. The signs are all there, waiting to be deciphered, but we're only just learning how to read them."

When I leave the store my mind is still filled with its images. As I look at the people passing me by on the street, I momentarily see the skulls behind their faces: this man's heavy supra-orbital ridge, that woman's delicate maxillae.

I realize that I am getting late for my lunch date with Hartley and hurry over to the Cuban-Chinese restaurant where we are meeting. I stop outside the restaurant to catch my breath and see him walking toward me, unnoticing, engaged in earnest conversation with himself. He looks so funny shaking his head and muttering away—something I have caught myself doing when I walk around the city by myself—that I smile broadly at him.

"We're very cheerful today, aren't we?" he says, ushering me into the restaurant and making a beeline toward the corner window table. People turn and stare at us as we pass, but I know it's not me they're looking at. Hartley is extraordinarily beautiful, a distillate of the best features of several races. He's tall and slim with long, shapely hands, olive skin, high cheekbones and almond-shaped eyes. Both men and women fall

madly in love with him, though he prefers men.
"Women spoil the fun," he is given to say. "They
always want to be told how pretty they look." I like
him despite this sort of nonsense and his affected ways.

After we order, Hartley immediately launches into
a detailed description of his many love affairs without
asking me anything about myself. He tells me how he
"turned around, so to speak" this fellow who lived
with his girlfriend but he soon got bored with the guy's
guilt-ridden whining. His latest boyfriend, a designer,
has promised to take him to Paris and launch him on a
modeling career.

"How long do you plan to keep this up?" I ask him.

"As long as I can get away with it."

"You know what I mean. You're too smart to just
spend your whole life being someone's kept man, letting people take you around like some exotic pet."

"Excuuuuse me," he says angrily. "What are you
doing with your life that's so great? Searching for
God?"

"That's right, you fucker. Someone has to do it."

We glare at each other for a moment and then burst
into hysterical laughter.

"That's a good one," he says, meditatively cutting
into the garlic-smothered pork chop the waiter has just
delivered. "The white girl goes in search of God."

By the time we do part, I am tired of him and his
jokes about whether I will still talk to him after my
canonization, but I am hurt, too, when he blithely tells
me that he probably won't have time to see me again
before he leaves for Europe in a week or so. I walk
away feeling that here is another failure in my human
relationships, that someone I have spent many late
nights exchanging my most secret thoughts with and
who I know through and through is still incapable of
taking me seriously.

I walk over to Riverside Park and continue uptown

along its central path. The sun is out at the moment and so are the people. Here, a young father squats to slip a baby carrier on his back, the child's head lolling to one side as it drools in pleasant sleep. There, two teenagers practice wheelies and rapid, skidding turns on their bicycles. On the grass, a tanned and shirtless man leans over his companion, his hand slowly stroking the smooth bare flesh of her upper arm. I also lie down and idle away my time, chewing on the sweet, white heart of a stalk of grass and letting myself be hypnotized by the endless variety of the parade. Every place has its ambient rhythm that draws you in until you become simply a part of its ebb and flow, like a sea anemone waving its tentacles in the tide. In California, you achieve this state of unexamined existence by driving along a coastal highway with the radio on loud. In New York, it happens when you fall into mindless reverie and let yourself become inseparable from the coursing crowd. It is easy for me to let this feeling take over, but afterward I am spent and more alone than before. I fear this commonplace alienation; I fear that I am destined to be mediocre no matter how much I fight it.

Clouds intermittently block out the sunlight and the light breeze is chillier than I had thought, so I move on toward the café where I will be meeting Mark later. On the corner of 106th, a man whose face is lit with the beatific nullity of the truly faithful hands me a pamphlet with the bold headline: WHERE WILL YOU SPEND ETERNITY?

"Behold, the bush burned with fire, and the bush was not consumed," he calls after me. Yes, I've felt that way too. Farther on, a frighteningly thin black man with a large hand-printed sign dangling from his neck waves a coffee cup at me. "*Sei gesund,*" he says as I drop a quarter into the cup.

At the café, I give my name and order to the pretty

but far-too-cool waitress who offhandedly writes it down. I sit at the table nearest the open door and spread my bag, books, and papers around so as to discourage anyone from sitting beside me. This place is filled with students and with regulars who tend to be excessively friendly and inquisitive. Something in the chi-chi system of having the waitresses call one's name out loud, perhaps, makes the people here feel more free to intrude. The best thing about this place is that they let you sit here as long as you like, no matter how small your order.

A woman comes in with two small children, a boy and a girl, who stand at the open door blowing bubbles while she is at the counter. The girl dips her bubble-spoon into the solution and is about to make a bubble when the boy says, "Don't blow yet. We'll do it together." He dips, purses his lips, raises the bubble-maker to his mouth. I watch as a drop of liquid forms at the base of the girl's bubble-maker and the thin membrane of soapy liquid breaks unnoticed.

"Now," says the boy. She blows; nothing happens. Her brother blows a beautiful iridescent bubble that is picked up by the wind and dances by my table.

"Isaac. Mark," the waitress calls. I glance around eagerly, pleased that my lover has arrived early, but I don't see him anywhere. "Mark," the waitress calls again. The man who raises his arm in answer is fortyish, balding; he wears a rumpled, button-down Oxford dress shirt. I watch as he takes a hurried sip of his coffee, his eyebrows comically raised as he blows steam into his face. I want to shout at him: "You're not my lover. Who do you think you are?"

The hours weigh heavily on me. I hate my job and yet days off are so dissatisfying, the time too limited but not finite enough, not sufficiently measured to press you into accomplishing anything. I find myself

counting the paintings of angels hung on all four walls
of the café. There are nineteen of them and they all
have the same face, which I realize, as I examine one of
the angels closely, is that of the Greek proprietor who
is sitting in the far corner. Either he could not find a
woman who was willing to model for him, or he likes
being surrounded by multiple images of himself. I
have never wished that the whole world were like me
... although I have wished that I were someone else,
sometimes *anyone* else.

Again I try to read, but Celan seems more obscure
than ever, even the poems I know well. Perhaps my
trouble concentrating is because I have strained my
eyes working at the computer terminal all week. If you
stare too long at a fixed distance, the muscles that allow
you to focus stiffen. Kate showed me an exercise to
"limber up" these eye muscles, and I decide to give
it a try. I take a red pen from my bag and hold it at
arm's length, while I hold my regular black pen
about six inches from my face. When I focus hard on
one of the pens, the other blurs into two images. I can
feel the eye muscles working as I shift focus, hold it,
shift again.

"Excuse me, what does this action mean?" a heavily
accented voice asks from somewhere behind me. The
inquirer turns out to be a psychologist from Prague
who is on a Fulbright to Columbia. He is mysterious,
shy, and very attractive. Besides, I'm a sucker for foreign accents. He asks me to have dinner with him and
we exchange phone numbers. The day is brightening
up, after all.

A few moments after my Czech goes back to his own
table, Mark comes in. He smiles at me and goes to the
counter, where he orders a "decapitated espresso."
The sultry waitress who wouldn't acknowledge my existence when she took *my* order is all smiles and ani-

mation for him. I feel a strong urge to throw something large and heavy at the both of them.

"Do you like bells?" Mark asks me when he sits down.

"Yes, I wear them on my fingers and toes, don't you know?"

"Silly. There's a special performance of the carillon at Riverside Church at three-thirty today. If we leave soon, we'll just catch it."

We finish up our coffee, Mark grabs both checks and pays, and we go outside. A strong wind has sprung up and brooding thunderclouds race across the sky. "Isn't the weather exciting," I cry, and Mark chuckles indulgently.

As we walk up Broadway, Mark looks with recognition at an elderly couple who are coming our way, clutching onto their hats and each other. Mark lived in this neighborhood for six months when he first came to the city and often says he would like to move back here.

"How are you, Mr. Vlaso? Mrs. Vlaso?" he asks. "How's the pharmacy doing?"

"Gone," the old man says. The couple resemble each other; they are white-haired, bowlegged, their faces set in an attitude of complaint. "The landlord raised the rent so he could get rid of us. Now he's put in a boutique." He pronounces the word *bo-teek*.

"That's awful," Mark responds.

"It's the most terrible thing that's ever happened to us. I don't know how we're going to survive it." He says something to his wife in a foreign language, links his arm with hers, and they cross the street.

"Unbelievable," Mark murmurs angrily. "You know those two survived a concentration camp together. Mr. Vlaso told me he used to go hungry for days just so he could bribe the kapos to let him stand near the fence where he *might* see her go by. He said it

only took a glimpse of her among a whole column of
women to give him the strength to stay alive. And now
they're being destroyed by a boutique! It's worse than
tragic, it's just stupid.''

I tried to imagine feeling that kind of devotion,
where someone else would be my reason for survival,
but I just couldn't see it for myself. And my sympathy
for the old couple felt out of place, too; their problems
have too real a source, they need not think themselves
self-indulgent for being miserable. Mark, however, has
no difficulty being indignant on their behalf and he
continues his monologue on the ravages of ''gentri-
fuckation.''

''You'd move in here if you could,'' I say to him.
''That's what happens: things change, there's progress, no one can stop it.''

''*I* would be perfectly content to shop at the local
bodega,'' he responds angrily. ''I don't need a Steve's
Ice Cream or a Café Pertutti.''

''Yes, but you'd pay a higher rent than some poor
Puerto Rican family could afford. So you're still part
of the problem....'' Really, why must he always be
better than everyone else?

''Okay, I'm responsible for the Vlasos' being out on
the street. Why don't we go back and find them so I
can give them a kick for good measure?''

We walk on in angry silence. The weather mirrors
our emotions; thunder growls menacingly in the distance and the wind spitefully whips particles of dust
into our eyes.

''Yeah, I guess we all take the food out of each other's mouths,'' Mark says after a while. ''Like my students say: it's a doggy dog world.''

''So you admit I've got a point?''

''Yes.'' He links his arm with mine. ''Bitch.''

A piece of newspaper blows against Mark's leg and

clings there while he frantically tries to kick it off. The sky darkens perceptibly, there is an unusually loud peal of thunder, and sharp pinpoints of rain stipple our backs. "Let's run," Marks says, having eventually gotten rid of his papery succubus. We cover the last hundred yards to the church just as the rain begins to lash the streets in earnest. We rush inside, and breathlessly pay our quarters to the cheerful, roundfaced man at the information desk before hurrying to the elevator.

I brush water off the fringe of hair hanging over Mark's forehead and he leans forward to kiss me. Just then the elevator stops and a short woman with a colorful South American shawl gets in. Her face has an almost Incan or Aztec cast to it, as if she had suddenly been transported here from Cortez's time. She has to stand on tiptoe to press the next-to-last button.

"Do you live here?" Marks asks. The woman smiles in incomprehension and says nothing. When the doors open for her stop, the flood of sound is deafening. "Do the bells disturb you in the morning?" he shouts, still not willing to give up communication.

The woman looks at us searchingly, then beams. "Tomorrow is every day," she enunciates as the doors slowly close.

"If we could only figure out what she meant by that," I say. For some reason this encounter has made me feel joyfully happy, as if I'm poised on the edge of an adventure.

"I'd forgotten this was a Shelter church," Mark says, almost to himself.

As we climb the rickety stairs to the bell tower, it is as if the sound of the bells is air or a liquid that is everywhere at once. The noise seems to have nothing to do with the comically tapping clappers and cantilevered mallets, the moving lines of bells. It swells up

from nowhere, is immanent in ourselves and the surrounding atmosphere. At one of the upper levels is the
booth where the carillonneur, a gnomelike man with
sparse tufts of graying hair, is frenetically pushing
and pulling at chocks of wood.

"Look," I yell. "It's God. He's pulling the strings
of the universe."

The little man is working awfully hard; beads of
sweat trickle down his face and neck as his feet pump
at the pedals and his hands fly over the pegs. He is
oblivious of the fact that he has an audience, is totally
caught up creating this melody that swells around us
and now begins to slowly fade. Finally, the carillonneur stops and wipes his forehead with the back of his
hand, then dries his hands on a ragged towel that lies
beside him on his bench. For a moment it is hard to tell
that the bells have stopped; my whole body still vi-
brates and there is a steady droning in my ears.

I go over to the large bell that is closest to me and
knock hard on it with my knuckle. Of course, it makes
no sound. Written on the plaque near it are the words
The inscription cast into this bell reads:

O YE ANGELS OF THE LORD
BLESS YE THE LORD PRAISE
HIM AND MAGNIFY HIM FOR-
EVER

The plaque goes on to tell us that at 20,510 pounds this
is the fourth-largest bell in the carillon and the musical
note it sounds is "E." Aside from the bell's outstanding size, it resembles the one we had hanging in the
front porch of the California house.

The string of small bells above our heads begins to
move and there is a pleasant trilling which rises to a
crescendo as all around us wires tug at levers and clappers strike. I notice that Mark has started up the last

set of the stairs leading to the top of the church tower and I follow him. There are puddles of water everywhere and the wind soughs at the lookouts, vying for our attention with the bells beneath our feet. Sudden gusts grasp at my dress and roughly tug at my braid. I pull out the barrettes and bobby pins, toss my head so my long hair falls around my shoulders, and laugh like a Victorian madwoman. I walk quickly once around the partly enclosed tower, then stop to watch as invisible hoofs stampede across the surface of the river below. In stories, this is when the revelation would happen. There would be a flash of divine light and everything would suddenly come clear. But this is now, today is today, and there are no more epiphanies: the loaves remain loaves and the fishes stay fishes.

We are the only ones here. I look over at Mark, who looks ruggedly handsome with his face flushed by the wind and his hair tousled. He moves toward me with a slight smile on his face. Nimble hands slip inside my dress and caress me, a warm mouth explores my throat and I feel the scrape of his rough beard. The wind howls around us; then, above it, we hear the deep bass questioning of the giant bourdon, the largest bell in the carillon. The smaller bells chime out their answer but it eludes me. There is no language, only sound, the imposition of a lover's hands, the impassioned roar of the elements, the strange wild coursing of my blood.

TEMPORARY SOJOURNER

He felt cramped, irritated, restless to an absurd degree. The air-conditioning had dried out his sinuses and made them ache, and the thought that the seemingly endless flight would actually be over in two hours did little to alleviate his present discomfort. It was close to fifteen years since Roger had last set foot in Johannesburg and he would have liked to be rested and alert, able to appreciate his return to the city of his birth.

Roger had not been able to sleep on the flight, although he had tried a number of times. He had felt out of sorts for the past two weeks; unbalanced by the break in his usual routine. He seemed incapable of focusing his thoughts. When he closed his eyes, his mind was assailed by a jumble of images—brief scenes and phrases from his childhood. He had not thought about his mother very often since her death two years earlier, but now memories of her came to him with regularity. He saw her as he had seen her when he was a child: tall, imposing but gentle, the motes of sunlight from the French windows illuminating her from behind and irradiating her hair. He heard her, too: a disembodied voice on the telephone, calling from Terre Haute, Indiana, where she had retired to live with her younger sister, also a widow. A series of illnesses had aged his mother fast, and in her later years her mind had begun to falter. Talking to him, she would lose track of her words and break into German, forgetting that he could not understand. German had never been spoken at home during his childhood, and, if the country itself should crop up in conversation, it was not mentioned as having any connection with her. Until a schoolfriend pointed it out, young Roger had not been aware that his mother had a slight tinge to her voice, an accent. In old age, her mother tongue had resurrected itself.

When Roger returned to New York from his mother's funeral, he brought back with him an aging leather briefcase bearing the tag: "Schönheim letters." The briefcase had lain unsorted, half forgotten in a closet until the time came for him to clear out storage space for his subletters while he was working in South Africa. Roger had finally opened the briefcase to see whether there was anything in it worth saving, whether it should be stored or discarded completely. He found a variety of yellowing papers inside: certificates of immigration, letters to landlords and businesses, photographs of his mother with friends or cousins whose pictures he had seen before but whose names he could not remember. He examined these things with only mild interest at first, then with increasing curiosity. For several hours, he sat carefully reading each letter and trying to decipher the dates and inscriptions on the backs of photographs. He wondered about the smil-

ing, hopeful young woman portrayed in these old snapshots—was this really the same person as the dis-
heartened widow who had brought him up?

One paper in particular unsettled him, although he
could not say for sure why this was so. It was an essay
his mother had written when she was around his present age of twenty-nine, a year before his birth and
almost nine years before her husband had died quietly
of a heart attack in the middle of a card game. Written
in ink on the torn-out sheets of an exercise book, the
passage hinted at a sense of inevitability that eluded
him. Roger had little time for the past; he saw it as
something left behind, that was all. He knew the author
of this essay only as his mother, a role that had always
seemed comforting to them both. In his mind he also
knew that she had had a life distinct from this relationship, but he had not been faced with so clear a
manifestation of this before. It left him with a vague
uncertainty.

Roger tried to sleep several times, but with little
success. He had brought the essay on the plane with
him and he decided to read it over again.

*My father was a tall man of stern appearance and
kindly nature. He dressed perfectly; even at home he
would wear a waistcoat and a smoking jacket. He wore
a gold chain across the middle of his waistcoat and
when, as a little girl, I was upset because I had been
slighted or had fallen, he would unfasten this chain
and let me examine the gold watch at the end of it. It
was a beautiful watch, fat, with a round face and
Roman numerals large enough for me to read, and if
he pressed a certain knob the watch would chime me-
lodiously, giving the hour. Then, when Jews were not
allowed any longer to own gold, this watch went the
way of our rings, necklaces, and other ornaments. They*

were very poor alchemists, those National Socialists,
turning fine gold into a mixture of pig iron and
chrome. For they did give my father a watch "in ex-
change"... one made out of less precious material,
suitable for a railwayman or a street cleaner, not a
businessman who could speak five languages. You can-
not escape fate, they told him. They were still being
polite then, and the man who came to collect the last of
our valuable things was apologetic.

We escaped, of course, and came here. I found a job
and married an Englishman with a big moustache who
I love very much. My sister married a visiting Ameri-
can, an engineer, and they have gone "to live in the
land of the red Indians."

Two weeks before my wedding, my father took a
shortcut through Highlands North Park, as he often
did. It began to rain and he stopped for shelter under
the huge oak tree on top of the hill. The steel watch was
melted like sealing wax by the lightning that killed
him.

Afterwards, I could not feel the same about this
warm country with its bright face full of promises. The
fate I thought I left behind in Germany has followed
me here; I can feel its shadow behind me.

It was a pity that there were no photographs of his
grandfather among the old papers. Roger had a clear
recollection of the sepia-toned photo portrait, safely
encased in a heavy steel-and-glass frame, that had for
years sat firmly on his mother's dressing table. This
picture had shown his grandfather to be a confident-
looking, sharp-featured man with thick, dark hair that
was cropped short. Roger's mother, on the other hand,
was delicate-featured and had always borne a slightly
haunted look. She believed, in a nonassertive way, in
tea-leaf readings and Tarot cards and had often told

him that destiny was the greatest existing natural force, that our lives would all be enriched if we would only pay heed to the signs that foretold our future. Although there was no great harm in her ideas, Roger could remember his mother breaking off her soliloquizing to him with a guilty start if her husband came into the room.

Roger had never been able to see the point of trying to read the patterns of clouds—except, perhaps, as harbingers of the day's weather. Even if the uttermost secrets of our existence *are* contained in the swirl of leaves at the bottom of a teacup, we cannot decipher them anyway, so why waste the time? He prided himself on being of practical mind, concerned only with the things that were not beyond his grasp, and as a consequence, he had done rather well for himself. The pattern of *his* life could be clearly plotted out, at least. There had been a brief time in his boyhood when adjustment had been a trial and he had felt out of sync with the world, but this was natural: getting used to having only one parent and living in an alien continent were things that would take their toll on anyone. The later steps had been relatively smooth; even majoring in art history had not had any negative effect on the course of his development, despite its not being the ideal educational background for a business that dealt primarily in share options and mineral rights.

The world had not thrown itself at his feet, but neither had it barred its doors to him—hard work and diligent application had been rewarded by a rapid rise in his position in the company that was now sending him to explore new avenues of investment in the land of his boyhood. With financial success had come renewed confidence and the loss of his youthful shyness. He had had lovers and fine evenings dining by candlelight, had rowed a boat for a young girl with soft hair

who had let her fingers trail in the rippling water, and
had made love to a sophisticated businesswoman whose
theater dress lay indifferently crumpled in a corner of
the room. He had no doubt that before too long he
would meet the right woman and settle into marriage,
providing the son he would have with the stability that
he had been denied.

Roger awoke to see the lengthened shadow of the jet
skirt across the tarred runway—looking not unlike the
passing swoop of a giant hawk—as they landed at Jan
Smuts.

"I hope you remembered to turn your watch back
twenty years," Amos Botha joked. He had kept up a
continuous stream of banter and information since
meeting Roger at the airport. Roger, who was wearing
a lightweight Brooks Brothers suit, felt out of place
beside the sprawling South African whose hirsute legs
jutted massively from a pair of khaki safari shorts.
Mossie was a mining-industries rep; Roger's local contact with the industry and an acquaintance who had
once or twice stayed with him at his apartment in New
York. Mossie had insisted that he be allowed to recip-
rocate until Roger was settled in Johannesburg.

"You're on home turf now, mate," he said, tapping
Roger on the knee with his large-knuckled, freckle-
covered hand. "I'll bet things have changed since you
lived around here, but don't worry, we'll make a regular *outa* of you yet. Pretty soon it'll be as if you never
left."

Mossie seemed too large for the Honda that he was
driving, and Roger found himself repulsed by the ginger-colored hairs that curled the length of the man's
bare legs and by his bluff manner. Mossie had not
seemed much different from the other businessmen
Roger knew in New York ... perhaps a little more
open, warmer. But, here, all traces of reserve were

gone, and Mossie had the patrician air of one introduc-
ing a newcomer to a country club or some selective
fraternity. Roger was unsure why he felt so intense a
craving for solitude. True, it had been a great many
years since he had lived here and he felt the garrulous
driver's presence as an intrusion on his testing the tone
and texture of this new world against the very memories it revived. His attention would have just focused
on a giant mulberry tree growing in a yard alongside
the road when Mossie would direct him to look at a
distant building silhouetted against the late-afternoon
sky.

"You're looking at the most modern skyline in the
whole of Africa," Mossie said, unconsciously reproduc-
ing almost the exact words and indicating much the
same vista as appeared on the back cover of his company's annual report. "This has got to be the most
beautiful country in the world. And I can say that
because I've been to every spot in the tourist books and
even a few that you wouldn't find in the encyclopedia.
None of them match up."

Roger tried to suppress the growing irritation Mossie's voice induced in him, and he realized that his
responses to his host's pleasantries might seem curt. It
must have been jet lag that was undermining his temper and judgment this way; he knew that much of the
respect the senior partners had for him was due to his
not being moody or easily ruffled. "A solid man," he
had overheard one of them say in reference to him, a
comment that filled him with satisfaction.

They drove into the city and out again, coming to a
suburban neighborhood with wide roads lined on either
side by tall jacaranda and oak trees. In this area it was
already dark, the trees growing so luxuriantly that
they filtered out most of the last rays of light from the
dying sun.

Mossie swung sharply into a Slasto-lined driveway,

shut off the engine, and jerked on the emergency brake.

"This," he said, "is where we will camp for the night."

The night was filled with a sweet, heavy scent as flowers emitted their last gush of fragrance before closing their buds until morning, and the dark trees were suffused with the murmur and rustle of settling birds. Roger took his ease on a swing chair on the Bothas' veranda, his hand clasped around a fat-bellied glass that housed the last third of his scotch-and-soda. There was just enough of a chill in the night air to be refreshing, and he felt revived by a shower and shave. A silk dress rustled behind him as Mossie's wife, Zelda, came out onto the veranda.

"I hope that you're not too tired to stand having guests at dinner tonight. We made the invitations so long ago, we just couldn't put them off."

"That's all right," he replied. "I feel fine. A little punchy, maybe."

She laughed softly at this, and Roger was pleased to note that her laugh lacked the nasal quality of her voice. Hers was an accent that would take a while to get used to: a flat, almost whining tone and the occasional consonant rasping, not unlike the sound of a hand plane shaving a block of hard wood.

Zelda perched on the railing to his right. She showed no concern for her long colorful evening dress, except to hitch it slightly at the knee.

"It's beautiful here, isn't it?" she said, her voice mingling wonder and assertion.

Roger agreed. *She* was beautiful. The cloth outlined the lithe, shapely lines of her body without either revealing or fully concealing them. When he and Mossie had arrived at the house, she had come bounding out to kiss her husband; her body, sheathed in a black swimsuit, streamed water, and her hair was hidden by a towel that was piled high like some ancient elaborate coiffure. He had not paid much attention to her then, although her handshake had left a few drops of cool water in his palm. Now she sat beside him, the silky tresses of her long hair cascading over her shoulders. They were silent; caressed only by the jasmine-scented night. Nearby a woman could be heard calling to her servant: "Francina. *Fran*cina. FRANCINA!" There was a brief pause during which the night reasserted itself, then came the slow, deep, leisurely reply: "M*iii*ssis?"

From somewhere else, farther away, a musical hum of voices singing along with a radio tuned to a Bantu station wafted over to where they were sitting. Then, the tinkle of ice against glass as Mossie came out onto the porch, bearing in either hand a freshly poured drink.

"It is like discovering that your mother is small-minded, deluded, even malicious," Roger was saying. "That does not mean that you can abandon her. Or turn her over to the authorities to be punished. Morally, maybe you should, but what sort of person lives by such abstractions?"

"Yes, that is exactly the point! That is why it is such a bloody tragedy that so many of the decent brains are running off to other countries like frightened schoolboys."

Roger looked with distaste at the squat fellow with horn-rimmed glasses who had just made this remark. He was wearying of the discussion and it distressed him to have these smug and clearly narrow-minded suburban people agreeing with all his statements. Worse still was to have his own ideas come tripping complacently out of the others' mouths. And he himself had talked too much until his voice had begun to sound hollow in his own ears ... though he had been rewarded by one or two quick smiles from Zelda. He had considered pointing out the irony of discussing the native question while the African servant brought around plates piled high with steaming food, but he had refrained.

Roger was glad when Horn Rims, who was entirely too self-possessed and possessive of the women around him, stood up and exclaimed: "Ag, I have had too much of your good wine and your good food." He squeezed Zelda's upper arm playfully and added, "So now I'll go home and have too much sleep, hey!"

The other two couples decided to depart as well, leaving Mossie, Zelda, and Roger to survey the damage. Dessert plates, napkins, cigarette stubs, and smudged wineglasses formed a jumbled collage on the dining-room table. The servants had left earlier, after receiving the injunction to make sure that everything was spick-and-span by breakfast time. Mossie went out of the room to get a bottle of Cape brandy, Réservée Speciale, to celebrate the occasion. Roger took the moment to smile at Zelda through hooded sleepy eyes. She gave him a puzzled glance and made the observation that he looked worn out and had better get to bed soon.

A woman's shrill cry interrupted them as they sat in the living room and talked. Mossie slammed his brandy snifter on the table beside him and strode angrily toward the front door. Roger followed him, and they stood together in the darkness of the front porch, listening. There was a heavy thump—like the sound of a carpet being strenuously dusted—and again the cry.

"My husband, you are killing me."

Mossie stepped forth into the darkness, shouting loudly. "Minna! What the hell is going on?" Roger followed. In the obscurity of the front lawn, he could barely make out two intertwined figures.

"Master. This is a bad woman." The voice was deep, resonant, unmistakably African.

"Why is she bad, Ivan?" Mossie spoke calmly, but there was an edge to his voice.

The African shrugged his wide shoulders. Then he remarked in a conversational tone, "She is very, very bad. A bad woman." The thought of her wickedness caught him short. He turned and thumped her on the back with his fist, whereupon she began to make a high keening sound.

"Stop that!" Mossie roared.

"She drink-it my money...."

"I don't want to know what this is about. I am not interested, do you hear? You have made a big noise and disturbed everybody! And you know you are not even supposed to be here, Ivan."

Zelda came up to Mossie and handed him a flashlight. He shone the beam on the figures crouched before him. The maid's large breasts hung loosely out of her torn uniform; as the light fell on her, she raised the pitch of her wailing. Ivan began a detailed explanation as to why he had not been able to return to the township that night.

"Enough!" Mossie exclaimed, raising his hand as if to guard against the onslaught of noise. "If you want to stay here, fine. Just be quiet. And if the police catch you because of all the bloody racket you are making, that's none of my business, understand?"

Ivan understood. His wife was a bad woman but he would see that she behaved and did not disturb the boss's sleep. There would be no more noise. To prove his point, he cuffed her on the head and her crying ceased abruptly. She stood up and began to weave her way toward her quarters in the backyard.

"You go to bed too, Ivan. If you don't hit your wife, maybe she won't drink so much, hey?"

"That was a good joke, baas," Ivan laughed in exaggerated appreciation and turned to follow his wife.

" 'Mos handled that very well," Roger said to Zelda as they walked back to the house.

"You get used to it," she replied.

Once inside the house, however, Roger felt the realization of how much he had had to drink well up in him. He had been shivering slightly in the chill outside, and the warmth of the house struck him unpleasantly.

"I'll be back in a minute," he muttered, groping his way toward the bathroom.

At eye level, inscribed in elegant blue lettering on the neck of the white porcelain bowl, is the word Standard. It takes a moment for Roger to focus on the letters, which do a blurry dance in synchronization with his receding waves of nausea. Standard what? His mouth tastes foul, and he spits, a long thread of mucus connecting him to the murky bowl below. His temples throb, and sweat breaks out on his back and burning forehead. Then, miraculously cool, wonderfully soft hands are stroking and soothing his aching head.

"Zelda," he murmurs, putting the weight of all his love and desire on those two syllables.

The hands flinched, almost letting his head drop forward against the white porcelain. Mossie's voice boomed from several inches behind his head, "Zelda, he's all right. Just make sure that there's some fresh coffee on the boil." Addressing Roger, he said gently, "Try to throw up again, man. It'll make you feel a lot better."

Roger rasped; his stomach was now emptied and

nothing came of it, although he could still feel the occasional peritoneal tremor. He clambered to an upright position, turned both the faucets on, rinsed his mouth, and furiously splashed water on his face.

"I'm a damn fool, Mossie," he said. "And I'm really sorry."

"Don't worry about it. It's my own fault for filling you with drink instead of letting you rest after your long flight. After a good night's sleep, we will all have forgotten about it."

Or we will pretend as if we did, Roger thought in a sudden access of embarrassment.

Outside in the moonlight, Ivan is creeping along on all fours. He has a colorful handkerchief tied around his head in the manner of a pirate. A gleaming ax is strapped to his belt. He crawls past Mossie's bedroom and stops outside the nursery, where Roger lies in restless sleep. The ax has been honed until it is razor sharp, and there is a thin line of blood on Ivan's cheek where he tested the weapon's sharpness against his own beard. One brief, hard blow—as would split perfectly a single piece of round stove wood—was all that would be needed....

Roger awoke with a start. He felt sticky and unrested. It was absurd, but he was sure that he could hear drums. He lay still for a while, listening. The silence was so unlike the constant hum of traffic he was used to that for some minutes all he could hear was the ringing of blood in his ears. But, if he really strained, he could detect a steady metallic beat—the throb of a heart in a kettle.

They came like thieves in the night. Where had he heard that? The drums continued to beat. Distant huge metal drums, they prophesied doom. A call to the African people to rise up and destroy the oppressor.

Mad! He was completely mad. Mad to come back here, mad to wake up in a fearful sweat, mad to get drunk and ... He switched on the light. The room revealed itself to be empty, comforting. Formerly a child's nursery, perhaps it would soon be filled again with the stuffed animals and other paraphernalia of an infant's presence. On a half-filled bookcase, against a wall where representations of zebras and wildebeests chased each other unceasingly, there sat a large brass alarm clock. This was the obvious source of the metallic throbbing, each tick reverberating along the wooden board on which the cheap clock rested.

Roger gave a wry smile and switched out the light, but as he lay down again a half-formed image appeared in his mind and he remembered his dream ... the ax, the creeping figure. But was it just his dream, he wondered, or was the whole sleeping city blanketed by the same suffocating vision? He could feel sanity and perspective dissolving into the surrounding dark, madness seeping into his brain with each pulse beat. But in what was the madness: in starting up and searching the room in fear, or in going back to sleep and dismissing it all as a fantasy born of tiredness?

Mossie snores in his sleep. Once, he rolls over and lets his arm flop around the slim waist of his wife, but this position is not comfortable and he is soon again on his back. Roger sweats, and wills sleep to come. He is overtired and his brain will not relax. Tomorrow he will be exhausted, not good for anything. He tries to think of his childhood and the places he may want to revisit while he is here, but the only image that comes to him is of the servant's fat breasts flopping out of her dress as she wails in the torchlight. Ivan is asleep on

the floor of his wife's room. She is snoring drunkenly
on the narrow iron bed. Gigantic shadows play across
their faces as a moth tries to find its way out of the
hurricane lamp that lights the small room. Each beat
of its wings only brings it closer to the flame, until it
drops in a scorched heap. As if in sympathy with the
moth, the wick chooses this moment to sputter and go
out, plunging the entire world into darkness.

G L O S S A R Y

asseblief · *please*
bandiet · *criminal, derogatory term for common prisoner*
biltong · *dried strips of beef jerky*
bliksems · *scoundrels*
boer, boere (plural) · *derogatory term for Afrikaners*
braai · *barbecue*
dagga · *marijuana*
die Taal · *Afrikaans (literally "the language")*
doekie · *a cloth head covering*
drongos · *long-tailed flycatcher*
insluitings · *enclosures*
iNyanga · *shaman, witch doctor*
kaffir · *derogatory term for black*
kaffirtjie · *kaffir plus the affectionate diminutive suffix -tjie*

kraal · *stockaded village; cattle pen*
kwela-kwela · *police wagon*
lekker · *lovely, nice*
mielie pap · *maize porridge*
Mrobaroba · *Zulu game of strategy*
outa, ous · *guy, guys*
Rock · *derogatory term for Afrikaners*
roti · *Indian pastry filled with meat or vegetables*
shebeen queen · *woman who runs a speakeasy*
Sies! · *expression of disgust*
skrik · *fright, terror, take fright*
songololos · *African millipedes*
springhaas · *hare*
spruits · *stream, rivulet*
Suikerbossie · *protea, traditional Afrikaans song that
    compares a girl to that flower*
te vuil · *too useless (literally too dirty, disgusting)*
toktokkie · *tapping beetle*
tsotsi · *gangster, crook*
verdompte · *damn*
verkrampte · *cramped, holding rigid political views*
voetsek · *get lost (obscene)*
Yussus! · *Jesus! (exclamation)*

ABOUT THE AUTHOR

Tony Eprile grew up in South Africa, where his father was editor of the country's first nonwhite mass circulation newspaper, *Golden City Post*. He received an M.A. in writing from Brown University and has taught writing at Brown, Harvard's Kennedy School of Government, and several other universities, as well as at old-age homes and the state prison in Rhode Island. In 1983 he was awarded a creative writing fellowship from the National Endowment for the Arts, and he has been a writing fellow at Wesleyan Writers Conference, the MacDowell Colony, and Dorland Mountain Colony. He lives and writes in New York City.